The Emerald-eyed Cat Mystery

Nancy fought back a wave of panic. She couldn't give in to fear now; she had to escape and find out what had happened to Elena and Ricardo. She was safe from discovery for the moment, she realized—*but where was she?*

She'd stumbled through another secret panel. Beyond that, she had no idea whether she'd fallen on a ledge above another stone stairway, or if she was in a level passageway. She was almost afraid to move.

An icy chill ran down Nancy's spine as she realized just how alone she would be without her friends, and she shuddered.

What if she was trapped forever in this blackness? What if she couldn't find a way out?

Nancy Drew Mystery Stories

Available from Wanderer Books

NANCY DREW MYSTERY STORIES®

THE EMERALD-EYED CAT MYSTERY

by
Carolyn Keene

WANDERER BOOKS
Published by Simon & Schuster, Inc.

Copyright © 1984 by Simon & Schuster, Inc.
All rights reserved
including the right of reproduction
in whole or in part in any form
Published by WANDERER BOOKS, A Division of
Simon & Schuster, Inc.
Simon & Schuster Building
1230 Avenue of the Americas
New York, New York 10020

Manufactured in the United States of America
10 9 8 7 6 5 4 3 2
10 9 8 7 6 5   pbk
NANCY DREW, NANCY DREW MYSTERIES, WANDERER
and colophon are registered trademarks of Simon & Schuster, Inc.

Library of Congress Cataloging in Publication Data
Keene, Carolyn.
The emerald-eyed cat mystery.

(Her Nancy Drew mystery stories; #75)
Summary: Kidnapped while trying to investigate the
sinking of three freighters, Nancy finds herself on a
hacienda in Colombia, where with the help of two friends,
she tries to unravel the mysterious connection between
the sunken ships and the strange events at the hacienda.
[1. Mystery and detective stories. I. Title
II. Frame, Paul, 1913–   , ill. III. Series: Keene,
Carolyn, Nancy Drew mystery stories; #75.
PZ7.K23Em   1984   [Fic]   84-5232
ISBN 0-671-49740-5
ISBN 0-671-64282-0 (pbk.)

Contents

THE EMERALD-EYED
CAT MYSTERY

1

A Strange Welcome

"Nancy, I have a job for you," Mr. Drew told his eighteen-year-old daughter, a famous amateur detective. "Would you go to Phoenix and visit my old friend and client, Jules Johnson?"

The titian-haired girl smiled with an excited sparkle in her eyes. "I'd love to, Dad. What's it all about?"

"Several months ago, Mr. Johnson bought a lot of material for his textile company during a visit to South America," Mr. Drew explained. "The cargo was shipped to the United States on a freighter called the *Rayo del Sol*. The ship sank and he was reimbursed for his loss by insurance. However, he was very upset because he had handpicked the cloth and cannot readily replace it. Then he heard something that made him suspect there may have been something fishy about the sinking of the freighter."

Nancy looked at her father expectantly. "What was that?" she asked.

The tall, distinguished-looking lawyer leaned back in his chair and folded his hands behind his neck. "Shortly after they received the insurance money, the Johnsons took a Caribbean cruise on a ship named *Fiesta*. They talked about the *Rayo del Sol* to a crewman, who remembered having seen the ship shortly before it went down. As a matter of fact, the sailors of the *Fiesta* had helped in the search for the *Rayo's* crew."

"I still don't understand what you're getting at," Nancy declared.

"Well, it turned out that the *Rayo* sank just outside of Cartagena, Colombia, which was not one of the freighter's ports of call. The ship wasn't supposed to be anywhere *near* that city."

"It could have changed its schedule for some reason, couldn't it?" Nancy inquired.

"Yes, that's possible. But Mr. Johnson was curious and called me about it, wondering whether perhaps fraud was involved. I checked around and found that not only the *Rayo*, but two other cargo ships had sunk near Cartagena in the last six months, and none of them was supposed to have been there."

"I see," Nancy said thoughtfully. "Were they all registered by the same company?"

"No," her father replied. "I haven't been able to find any link there. I called MIC Transport Company, which owned the *Rayo*. A clerk told me the man in charge would return my call, but he never did. Subsequent calls were not even answered. I had no better luck with the other two companies. Why don't you see Mr. Johnson? Perhaps he can give you more information. Then I'd like you to go on to Los Angeles and interview the crew of the *Fiesta*. You may pick up a clue or two there."

Nancy stood up and raised her hand in a mock salute. "Yes, sir! When should I leave?" The prospect of another mystery to solve was exciting to her and she wanted to get started as soon as possible.

"How long will it take you to pack a suitcase?"

Nancy giggled. "Five minutes!"

"Ha!" her father teased. "A woman takes longer than that to pack a handbag! But let me call the airport and see if I can get you an afternoon flight."

When Nancy entered the Cafe del Pueblo in Phoenix the following day, she smiled as she recognized the middle-aged couple sitting at a corner table. The Drews had known the Johnsons for many years and she was glad to see them again. A moment later, however, she felt a slight wave of apprehension as she greeted her old friends. There seemed to be a strange lack of welcome on their part!

"Your father isn't with you, Nancy?" Mr. Johnson asked her with some hesitation.

"No, he'll be tied up in court for a few days," the girl replied. "But he's been investigating your case and wants you to know what he's learned so far."

"He could have mailed us a report," Jules Johnson declared. "He didn't need to send you all the way out here to deliver it."

Nancy laughed. "Actually, I'm only stopping briefly in Phoenix on my way to Los Angeles," she said. "That's why I suggested that we meet downtown rather than at your house in the suburbs. I'll be interviewing the crew of the *Fiesta*, since they were the ones who brought your attention to this mystery. I also want to contact several shipping companies while I'm there."

"*Several* shipping companies?" Mrs.

4

Johnson, a plump, gray-haired woman, frowned.

Nancy nodded. "When you telephoned Dad about the sinking of the *Rayo del Sol,* he checked with a number of insurance companies. He found out that the *Rayo* was only one of three ships that had sunk under similar circumstances." Quickly the young detective told the Johnsons what her father had learned.

Mrs. Johnson shrugged. "I don't know—the more I think about it, the more I feel we're making a mountain out of a molehill," she said. "The insurance was paid. We weren't defrauded."

"That's true," Nancy said. "But Dad tried to contact the owner of the *Rayo del Sol* several times, and didn't get an answer. It's very peculiar."

"Perhaps there aren't any answers," Mr. Johnson stated. "This could be a wild goose chase, Nancy. The *Rayo* may have picked up unscheduled cargo in Cartagena. I think we should forget the whole thing. After all, the insurance company didn't feel there was anything suspicious about the claim."

Mrs. Johnson nodded. "There's really no reason for you to go to California, my dear," she added. "Why don't you stay with us and enjoy Phoenix for a few days?"

5

Nancy put down the taco she was about to bite into and frowned. "Are you saying that you're no longer interested in knowing whether there was fraud involved in the sinking of the *Rayo del Sol*?" she asked.

Mr. Johnson shrugged. "It's a small matter. I was angry in the beginning, but I've been very busy the past few days and really don't want to pursue the investigation." His gaze went around the quiet garden cafe and Nancy followed his eyes, aware that the man was uncomfortable.

"I'm afraid I can't stop now," she said softly. "We've found too many suspicious coincidences and feel they warrant checking out. Of course, if I don't learn anything in Los Angeles, I suppose we'll have to give up." She smiled. "Perhaps I can stop and report to you on my way home? I'll only be in California for a night or two."

"I don't know if I'll be in town," Mr. Johnson replied evasively. "I have some pressing business that has come up suddenly."

Nancy glanced at Mrs. Johnson and saw confusion in the woman's face. Apparently she knew nothing about her husband's impending trip. The Johnsons were obviously very worried about something, and the young detective suspected that it had to do with her investigation.

6

Mr. Johnson quickly changed the subject. "How is Hannah Gruen?" he inquired. "Still taking good care of you and your father?"

Nancy smiled, allowing herself to relax a little as they talked about the Drews' kindly housekeeper and other friends that the Johnsons had in common with Nancy and her father. She didn't mention the mystery again until lunch was over and the couple was helping her into a taxi outside the cafe.

"There's really nothing more you can tell me regarding the *Rayo del Sol?*" she asked.

Mr. Johnson shook his head. "It's not important. But if you feel you must follow up this matter, just—just be careful." With that, he closed the cab door and walked away, his arm around his wife's shoulder.

Someone must have threatened him or warned him not to continue the investigation, Nancy thought. She looked out the window and saw a tall, dark man climb into a car on the other side of the street. He looked vaguely familiar. Had she seen him in the cafe? A moment later, the car vanished into the traffic and her taxi driver took her to the airport.

Nancy's flight to Los Angeles was a short one, and upon her arrival she checked into a nearby

7

hotel. After freshening up, she called a taxi to take her to San Pedro, where the shipping companies she wanted to visit were located. It was also the berthing place for the cruise ship *Fiesta*, which she was hoping to catch before it sailed on its next journey.

"Would you please take me to the MIC Transport Company on Third Street?" she asked the driver. She glanced back at the hotel entrance just in time to see the same tall, dark man she had noticed in Phoenix hurrying toward a gray sedan. Nancy frowned. Was this just another coincidence, or was the man following her?

Although the gray car went off in the opposite direction, when the taxi reached Third Street, the girl felt uneasy again. She found herself in a rundown harbor area with decaying warehouses and shuttered-up buildings.

Her driver stopped in front of one of them. "Seems you're out of luck, Miss," he said. "This place isn't in business any longer."

Nancy sighed, then consulted her list and gave him the second address. It was less than a block away, as was the third company. All the offices were dark, and CLOSED signs hung over their doors.

"Where do you want to go now?" the driver asked.

"Do you know where the *Fiesta* is docked?" the girl inquired.

He nodded. "Not far from here."

"Well, unless it has already sailed, I might as well go there," she decided, feeling bitterly frustrated.

"It just arrived today," the driver informed her. "You don't need to worry."

His words proved correct. The *Fiesta* was a huge, white ship buzzing with activity. It took nearly an hour before Nancy was able to talk to the busy captain. He summoned three sailors to his office. "Perhaps these fellows can help you," he said. "Most of the crew is new and wouldn't know anything about the *Rayo* sinking."

As the first man entered, the captain stood up. "You can talk right here," he said. "I have to go up to the bridge." With that, he left the office.

Nancy spoke to the young man, who was pleasant but could not give her any information. Neither could the second sailor, who arrived a moment later. "The *Rayo del Sol* was just another ship in port," he said. "I paid no attention to it until the rescue mission the following day. And at that point we really didn't talk to the crew; all we did was fish them out of the water."

The third man walked in just as the other two were leaving. "I'm Barry Cole," he said, after Nancy had introduced herself. He was slim and tall and appeared to be only a few years older than the girl detective.

"I understand you were on the *Fiesta* during a cruise several months ago," Nancy said. "When you stopped in Cartagena, Colombia, did you see the freighter *Rayo del Sol*?

"That's the ship that sank a day later, isn't it?" Barry asked.

"Yes."

"Sure, I saw it. Not only that, I visited it. I'm a language student, and whenever we were in a foreign port, I went ashore and practiced talking to the people on the docks and other ships, even if I only had a few minutes."

Nancy felt a surge of excitement. "What were they saying?"

"At first, the usual. But then one fellow told me he had overheard that the freighter was sailing with almost no cargo, and he couldn't understand why!"

10

2

Close Call

Nancy stared at Barry Cole in utter surprise. "You say there was hardly any cargo on the *Rayo del Sol* before she sank?"

Barry nodded.

"Did the man tell you anything else?" the girl pressed.

"Offhand, I don't remember. Look, I have to get to the airport. This was my last cruise; I'm going back to college. Do you want to come with me while I get my things? Maybe I'll think of something else that might be useful to you."

"I'll do better than that," Nancy said. "I'll go to the airport with you. We can share a taxi."

"Good idea."

A half hour later the two young people walked

off the cruise ship. Barry carried two large duffel bags and a suitcase. "We'll have to go to First Street to catch a taxi," he said. "I know a shortcut through the warehouse over there, if you don't mind."

"Of course not," Nancy assured him.

As they strolled through the bustling warehouse, Nancy suddenly stopped short.

"What's the matter?" Barry asked.

"There's a tall, dark man ahead of us," she said softly. "I saw him in Phoenix and again at my hotel in Los Angeles. I have a feeling he's been following me!"

Barry, who had heard about Nancy's detective work while he was packing his clothes, stared at the girl in surprise, then said, "Well, let's go after him!"

The two hurried through the aisles lined with heavy cartons and boxes. Suddenly, Nancy heard a rumbling to the left, and a stack of wooden crates began to rock violently. Instantly, she grabbed Barry's arm and dragged him away. A moment later, the huge crates toppled down behind them!

The roar of the crates exploding against the concrete was like thunder. Splinters of wood and pieces of metal flew through the air, some of them striking Nancy and Barry, driving them

12

farther into the shadows of the warehouse.

Finally they stopped running. "What in the world was that?" Barry gasped, trying to catch his breath. "If you hadn't dragged me away—"

Nancy's face was grim. "I don't believe it was an accident," she whispered. "Let's get away from here as fast as we can."

The two made their way out of the warehouse. Nancy paused only once to look back, trying to see if her pursuer was anywhere in sight. There was no sign of him, however, and soon the young detective and Barry Cole were on their way to the airport.

Barry could not add any clues when he tried to recall his conversation with the sailor on the *Rayo del Sol*.

"Apparently the insurance company did not hear about this," Nancy said thoughtfully, "or it would have investigated. If there was little or no cargo on the ship before it sank, it must have paid for claims that weren't justified."

"But then what happened to the cargo you say was supposed to have been on board?" Barry wondered. "And why did the ship come to Cartagena?"

"That's what I'll find out," the girl said with determination.

At the airport, she said good-bye to Barry, who promised to call her at home if he should think of anything else or hear more about the mysterious ship from his sailor friends. Then Nancy went to her hotel and called her father. She reported all that had happened, and Mr. Drew listened carefully.

"I think you should come home," he said.

Nancy was reluctant to admit defeat. "There's one more thing I can do while I'm here," she suggested. "I'd like to visit the dock employment office tomorrow and see if I can locate someone who was on the *Rayo del Sol* during that eventful trip."

Mr. Drew thought for a moment. "Okay," he said finally, "go ahead. Just be careful."

"I will, Dad," she promised.

The next morning the young detective arrived at the harbor bright and early, and went into the small office where sailors and dockworkers signed up for jobs. A middle-aged man sat behind a desk and looked at her curiously. "Do you want to sign up for a cruise?" he asked. "Are you an entertainer?"

Nancy shook her head and briefly told him what she needed to know.

The man stroked his chin. "I could go through

the files to see if I can find anything," he said. "But it'll take a while. Can you come back tomorrow?"

Nancy was disappointed about the delay, but knew she could not do anything about it. "Sure," she said, flashing a smile at the man. "I really appreciate your help."

She left the office, which by now was crowded with seamen. She did not notice one of them following her out until he tapped her lightly on the arm.

Nancy whirled around and stared into the eyes of a small Oriental man in overalls. A smile curled his pencil-thin mustache.

"I heard you talk to Roger in the office," he said. "Maybe I can help you."

Nancy's heart beat with excitement. "Were you on the *Rayo del Sol* when she sank?"

The man shook his head. "No. But a friend of mine was. He was one of the officers."

"Where can I find him?"

"In San Francisco. After the *Rayo* sank and he almost drowned, he decided he had had enough of the sea. He'd been saving his money for a long time, and he opened a restaurant on Grant Avenue in Chinatown."

"What's his name?" Nancy pressed.

The sailor pulled out his wallet and riffled

through some folded papers and credit cards. Then he pulled out a dog-eared business card and handed it to Nancy. "Here. He gave me this in case I wanted to visit his place someday. I know the address, so you can have it. His name is Jim Liu. Tell him Charlie Sim sent you."

Nancy pocketed the card and thanked the man. She debated whether she should speak to the employment agent again in the morning for further information or go to San Francisco right away to follow up her new clue. Quickly, she decided on the latter. An hour later she was at the airport.

As she hurried toward the terminal, she noticed a tall, dark man emerge from a car. It was ominously black with black-tinted windows that permitted the driver and passengers to see out, but no one to look in.

Nancy's heart pounded. Although she didn't recognize the car, she was positive that the stranger was the same man who had been stalking her every movement. She went into the building and quickly glanced up and down the row of ticket counters, observing the flight schedules overhead. One listed departures for New York.

I hope this works, she told herself, stepping into line. She reasoned that the man would see her and figure she was homeward bound. But what if he sticks around to make sure? I know, she thought. I'll buy a ticket for New York and go to the gate, if necessary. When the coast is clear, I'll return the ticket and buy one for San Francisco. Good thing I've got Dad's credit card with me!

The line was fairly long, and Nancy waited several moments before casually looking around her. When she did, she was surprised to see the stranger standing in another ticket line three rows away. A lump rose in her throat as she realized that *he* might be flying to San Francisco!

3

Happy New Year!

Nancy knew she had no choice but to stay where she was. Her line moved slowly, more so than the man's. He stepped up to the counter while Nancy was still waiting.

He'll probably buy his ticket, then head for the gate, she thought. But what do I do? Take the flight to San Francisco and wind up sitting next to him on the plane? No thanks.

Her line edged forward, giving her a better view of the man. He was arguing with the woman behind the counter, who tried to remain calm. Still, her expression revealed annoyance, and her lips tightened as the man finally bolted off to an exit and left the airport.

Although stunned by his unexpected departure, Nancy was also tremendously relieved.

She hurried over to the woman, glad there had been no one else in line behind him.

"May I help you?" the clerk asked her.

"That man certainly was rude," Nancy said, trying to draw out some information. The woman merely nodded. "I'd like a seat on the five o'clock flight to San Francisco," Nancy continued.

"Seems everybody wants one." The woman cocked her head toward the exit door through which the obnoxious man had left. "But there are no more seats available. That's why that man was so angry."

So he *was* planning to fly to San Francisco, the girl detective concluded. "Oh dear," she said aloud. "I really do need to get to San Francisco today. Is there another flight later on?"

"Just a minute. Let me check." The clerk pressed the keyboard on her computer terminal several times. "Here's something. There's one seat left on the eight o'clock. Is that okay?"

"Perfect," Nancy replied happily. "It's that or the bus," she added with a laugh, "but I don't have that much time."

The woman smiled as she wrote out the plane ticket and handed it to the young detective. "Enjoy your flight, Miss," she said.

"Oh, I will." Nancy glanced at the big clock in the middle of the terminal. It was only four-thirty; she would have to wait three hours before being able to board the plane. Should she go back to the city? It seemed wiser to stay.

She bought a couple of magazines and found a comfortable bench outside the security area. She sat there reading for nearly an hour, then abandoned her seat for a leisurely stroll. At last, it was seven-thirty, and Nancy headed for the boarding gate. The man was nowhere in sight, and her fears of being followed to San Francisco were diminished.

The flight proved as uneventful as the preceding hours, and it was only when Nancy stepped into the taxi outside the San Francisco terminal that her sense of urgency about the investigation returned.

"Please take me to Chinatown," she told the driver.

"Chinatown takes up about twenty-four blocks, young lady. Which one do you want?"

"I'll tell you in a second," Nancy said, digging into her purse for the business card Charlie Sim had given her. "Mr. Liu's restaurant on the corner of Grant Avenue and California Street."

"I'll do my best," the driver replied. "But I can't promise to take you right to the door. It's the Chinese New Year, and there's a big parade going on. The streets will be jammed with people."

"Well, then, let me off wherever you can," the young detective said. She sank back against the seat as the cab pulled away from the curb.

The hazy, soft light that had bathed her plane during lift-off in Los Angeles had faded into a cool, ink-blue sky that hung icily over the highway. The temperature was much lower than in Los Angeles, and Nancy, feeling chilled, was hoping that a walk through Chinatown would warm her up.

When the taxi reached the area, the driver dropped her off in front of a towering, pyramid-shaped building.

"Is this Grant Avenue?" Nancy inquired, squinting at a corner sign.

"No. But do you see that cable car over there? That'll take you where you want to go."

"Thanks," she said, as she paid him. She ran toward the cable car, which rapidly filled up, mostly with Chinese-Americans in attractive silk garb on their way to celebrate the New Year.

Nancy was one of the last to climb aboard, and as the cable car rumbled forward, the din of excited conversation grew softer. Up and down the steep hills, the cable car screeched along, stopping only occasionally to pick up more passengers. No one got off until the end of the line.

The sound of firecrackers and blaring music told her that the parade was less than a block away, and she trailed after the hurrying crowd.

Soon she was caught in the swell of people who jammed both sides of Grant Avenue, blocking entranceways to buildings. For an instant, the young detective was totally stymied. If only she knew the precise location of the restaurant. She pressed through the crowd, stepping into the protection of a doorway to look at the business card again.

Then she showed it to a woman in a green tunic dress who pointed to a pagoda-like structure far up the street. Its curling roof was lit up by small lights, indicating the restaurant was open.

Nancy thanked the woman and hurried to the restaurant. The small lobby was lacquered in red, and there was a narrow stairway that led up to a gold-trimmed door. When she opened it, a distinguished-looking gray-haired man greeted her with a bow.

"I wish to speak with Mr. Liu," Nancy said, observing the elegant, table-filled room beyond.

"I am Mr. Liu. And you are . . . ?"

"Nancy Drew," the girl replied. "Charlie Sim sent me."

"Yes, yes. Well, do come inside. You grace my humble establishment with your lovely presence, Miss Drew."

He ushered her past several patrons to a

corner secluded by a handsome silkscreen that served as a partition. Nancy was impressed by the man's polite manner and allowed herself to be seated before asking him any questions.

"Permit me to serve you dinner, Miss Drew," the proprietor said.

"But—"

"You are my guest, please," he interrupted, raising his hand in protest.

"But, Mr. Liu, may I speak with you first?" Nancy persisted.

"First you should dine." He smiled, excused himself, then returned shortly with a waiter and a plate of pan-fried shrimp. "Baked with sea salt," Mr. Liu announced, as the dish was placed in front of Nancy.

Next, he produced honeyed spareribs, followed by a delectable soup, and finally, the specialty of the house, Peking duck.

"Are you ready for dessert, Miss Drew?" Mr. Liu asked when she had swallowed her last mouthful.

"No, thank you," the girl replied, dabbing her lips with a napkin. "I'm really not used to such a feast."

"Ah, but it is the Chinese New Year, and you must eat a little of everything." Once more he signaled to the waiter, who brought a bowl of fresh fruit and a pot of jasmine tea.

"It was all so delicious," Nancy complimented Mr. Liu as he sat opposite her, pouring the tea.

"I'm honored you liked it."

"And the tea is wonderful," she said, taking a sip of the aromatic liquid.

"It makes you feel relaxed, so at peace with the world, doesn't it?" Mr. Liu remarked, fixing his eyes on hers.

"Oh, yes." The girl detective was unaware of the hypnotizing effect the man's stare had upon her. He began asking her questions in a low, soothing tone, and she responded openly. Without being aware of it, she revealed all the details of her mission to California. Mr. Liu told her that the *Rayo del Sol* had been loaded with cargo, contrary to the rumor she had heard. "We carried many things, among them bales of beautiful cloth," he said. "Too bad engine trouble caused the ship to sink."

The conversation went on for a long time, and at the end Mr. Liu said softly, "You will go back to River Heights, Nancy Drew, and forget about this investigation. You will also forget that I told you to return. You will only remember that you had an extraordinary meal. Do you understand?"

24

"I do." Nancy nodded obediently.

"Good. Now you may leave. And Happy New Year, Miss Drew."

When Nancy stood outside the restaurant, she inhaled the cool night air and felt the exhilaration of the parade-goers around her. They whistled and cheered as a large, colorful Chinese dragon marched past, pulling everyone along, including the young detective.

But soon the revelry ended and Nancy glanced at her watch. Nearly three hours had elapsed since she arrived in Chinatown. Where had the time gone? she wondered. Apart from the unusual meal she had enjoyed, she only remembered the thrill of the parade.

Nancy giggled. "Well, it doesn't matter," she thought. "All I want to do now is go home." As she knew there was no flight to Bayport this late, she started to call a taxi to take her to a hotel. Suddenly, she stopped short. A tall, dark man had slipped out of a doorway and crossed the street in front of her.

The sight of him jarred her memory. Nancy knew she had seen him before, but where? Danger! her subconscious flashed. He means danger!

25

4

Kidnapped!

Nancy tried to follow the man, but lost him. She left Chinatown and checked into a downtown hotel, then lay awake in her bed, trying to piece together the events of the evening.

Slowly, she began to remember what had happened. The dark man had been following her. Apparently he had managed to fly to San Francisco after all, perhaps on a chartered plane. Charlie Sim had sent her to see Jim Liu, who had set her mind at ease about the *Rayo del Sol.* But Mr. Sim was wrong! Had he misled her intentionally? "He must have!" Nancy spoke out loud and sat up in her bed. "He wanted me to go home and forget all about the ship. But I won't.

In the morning, I'll go back to the San Pedro employment office and see if Roger has found anything!"

But the personnel manager was not helpful when Nancy arrived there the next day. He told her curtly that he had not sent anyone to the *Rayo del Sol,* that its crew had been South American, and that he could not give her any more of his time. The girl was not sure whether he was telling the truth. Maybe someone had gotten to him, just as someone had threatened the Johnsons, she thought. And I'll have a better chance of finding out what's going on from *them* than from this stranger. Perhaps if I tell them what I've learned so far, they'll talk to me.

As soon as Nancy arrived in Phoenix she called the Johnson home.

"You're back so soon!" Mr. Johnson said with surprise when he heard her voice. "Does that mean you've decided to give up on this case?"

"Not exactly," Nancy replied. "I'd like to talk to you and your wife, if you have the time."

There was a moment of silence, then he said, "You're at the airport?"

"I have about two hours before my flight to River Heights leaves," Nancy replied.

"My wife isn't feeling well, but I'll be there as soon as I can." Jules Johnson didn't sound happy, and Nancy swallowed a sigh before she thanked him and arranged a meeting place.

She hung up the receiver, but didn't hurry to join the straggle of people moving toward the main terminal area. Aware that she would have at least half an hour before Mr. Johnson arrived, she strolled along the concourse, deciding that she'd spend the time looking for a book or magazine to read on her flight to River Heights.

As she stepped into the busy lounge, a man in a brown uniform came toward her, frowning slightly. "Miss Drew?" he asked. "Miss Nancy Drew?"

Nancy nodded, startled at being recognized, but also aware that her picture often appeared in newspapers when she and her father solved spectacular cases. "I'm Nancy Drew," she acknowledged.

"There is a call for you," the man said. "A most urgent call, the gentleman said." He smiled. "If you will follow me?"

It had to be her father, Nancy decided. Perhaps he'd made some exciting discovery since their last conversation, maybe even something that would change her plan to fly back to River Heights. The man indicated a door marked 'Private,' and Nancy hurried inside with a quick thank you. Her mind was so busy speculating about what her father might have to say, she did not notice the man standing behind the door. The next moment, she was struck by a sharp blow. She dropped into the silent darkness of unconsciousness without making a sound!

When Nancy regained her consciousness, her head was throbbing and the floor seemed to move. She tried to sit up to ease the pain in her back and shoulders, but her hands were numb, and when she attempted to move them forward, nothing happened. Slowly, she opened her eyes, but found only darkness.

A scream welled up in her throat, but no sound came out. Her tongue was dry and her mouth seemed full. It *was* full—she had been gagged! Her eyelashes brushed against fabric, revealing that her darkness was caused by a blindfold.

How did I get here? she wondered, squirming to a slightly more comfortable position. Then she remembered the Phoenix Airport, the uniformed man, the phone call . . . and the blow on her head.

The pain had receded a little, but the throbbing sound continued and Nancy realized suddenly that she was in an airplane. Shocked, she scrambled to sit up, then cried out as her head pounded, and she slumped back to the floor.

How had she gotten on this plane, and where was it taking her? Why was she bound, gagged and blindfolded?

There were no answers in the noisy darkness. Because of the physical strain she had been under, Nancy soon dropped into a kind of restless half-sleep. She was dreaming of the rocking crates and Mr. Liu, when something hit her side. She cried out in pain, a sound that the gag in her mouth stifled. She opened her eyes, and even though she was still blindfolded, the darkness that had surrounded her suddenly seemed much lighter.

"Who are you?" a feminine voice gasped, and Nancy felt soft fingers on her cheek as the blindfold was pulled away.

In the dim glow of a flashlight, Nancy saw a girl only slightly older than herself bending down. She had dark eyes and long, black hair. "What happened?" she asked, but the young detective could not answer until the stranger removed the gag from her mouth.

"Thank you," Nancy croaked, her mouth dry and sore from the fabric. "Where am I? What am I doing here? Would you untie me?"

"Who are you?" the girl repeated, as Nancy sat up and turned her back so the girl could see her hands. "How did you get on this plane?"

Nancy sighed, realizing they were getting nowhere just asking each other questions. "I'm Nancy Drew," she began. "I was in the airport in Phoenix when someone knocked me unconscious. When I woke up, I was on this plane. That's all I know." She let out a moan of mixed pain and relief as the ropes dropped from her wrists and she could bring her aching arms forward. "What about you?"

"My name is Elena Escobar," the girl answered in slightly accented English. "This plane belongs to my family."

"Where is it going?" Nancy asked.

"It is returning to the del Luz hacienda in the hills beyond Cartagena, Colombia," Elena replied. "Do you have any idea who put you here?"

Nancy shook her head. "I was hoping *you* could tell *me*," she said. "If the plane belongs to your family, shouldn't you know?"

Elena dropped her eyes and plucked nervously at her wrinkled jeans. "I—I'm not supposed to be here myself," she replied softly. "The pilot took me to Phoenix yesterday so I could return to Arizona State University. I was home for Christmas vacation."

"Then why are you here?" Nancy perservered.

31

"When I got back to school last night, I called my fiance, Ricardo, at home. We're to be married in the spring, as soon as I turn twenty-one. I was concerned about my aunt. She acted very strangely while I was home on holiday."

"Your aunt?" Nancy asked.

"Yes. She raised me like a daughter. My parents were killed in an accident when I was a baby, and Aunt Rosalinda and Uncle Jose brought me up. My uncle died about four years ago, and Aunt Rosalinda and I—" Her voice broke and tears rolled down Elena's cheeks. "I just never thought something like this could happen to us."

"What do you mean?" Nancy said.

"She acted as if I were her enemy all of a sudden. We used to be very close. I could talk to her about anything, and she'd tell me about the business, and trust me. But this time, when I came home, she treated me as a stranger. All of a sudden, she hates me!" Elena began to sob violently.

Nancy put an arm around the girl's shoulder. "There must be an explanation," she said. "I'm sure it has nothing to do with you personally. Someone must have intentionally turned your aunt against you."

Elena nodded. "Anyway, when I spoke to

Ricardo last night, he told me that Aunt Rosalinda had not left her room since my plane took off and that she refused to see him when he tried to visit her. Now she has turned against him, too!"

"Perhaps she just didn't feel well yesterday," Nancy suggested.

Elena shook her head. "That wasn't it. She made it very clear to him that she wanted nothing more to do with him. You must understand that my aunt is a wonderful person. She and Ricardo's father were great friends before he died. He managed the hacienda for her for many years, and even though Aunt Rosalinda now has another manager, she would always discuss things with Ricardo. But suddenly she's shut him out, as well as me."

Elena blew her nose and then continued. "After I spoke to him, I realized that something terrible may happen at home. I decided I had to go back to find out what, so I hid in the plane. No one knows I'm here."

Nancy nodded.

"I was shocked when I stumbled over you," Elena went on. "I don't even know who you are."

Nancy took a deep breath. Could she trust this girl? "I'm an amateur detective," she said. "I

33

was working on a case in Phoenix and was expecting to meet someone at the airport when I was conked over the head. The next thing I knew, I was on this airplane."

"Do you have any idea why?" Elena asked.

Nancy suspected it was related to her case. She was investigating ships that had sunk in Colombia, and now she was on a private plane, kidnapped, on her way to that country. But she did not want to reveal any details to Elena at this point.

"Not really," she answered. "It may have something to do with my investigation, but I don't know what. All I know is that I have to get away. Can you help me?"

"I will try," Elena promised. "If we can get off the plane unnoticed after it lands, I can hide you and make arrangements for you to fly back to the United States. I know my Aunt Rosalinda would never condone a kidnapping. We can—"

She was interrupted by a sound from beyond the door leading to the passenger area of the plane.

"Someone is coming!" Elena gulped. "I have to hide!"

5

A Spooky Hacienda

Elena stumbled to her feet and dived between the shadowy mounds of equipment that were stacked haphazardly in the cargo area of the airplane.

Nancy lay still. For a moment, she considered hiding, then realized the futility of such a move. Elena might be able to get away with it in the cluttered cargo bay, but only as long as no one was searching for her. Nancy had no such option. If she wasn't lying where the men had left her, they'd tear the plane apart until they found her.

She picked up the soggy gag, biting her lip at the thought of putting it back in. But the sound of the cabin door being opened spurred her into action. Quickly she retied the gag and pulled the blindfold over her eyes. There was no time to retie the ropes around her wrists, so she simply crossed her hands beneath her, hoping that whoever was coming would think she was still unconscious and not bother to check her bonds.

"Well, well, well, how are you doing, Miss Drew?" a man asked in Spanish as he stepped inside. "Having a nice trip?"

Nancy let her breath out slowly, forcing herself to relax, though every muscle in her body was tense. He came closer, his footsteps sounding loud and menacing over the steady beat of the engines. He stopped just inches away from her. It took all her self-control to keep her breathing steady, and she was grateful that the blindfold covered her eyes, otherwise he would have known that she was awake.

"Still out, huh?" The man continued. "Just as well, I suppose."

He bent down and Nancy shuddered as his rough fingers pushed her hair aside and checked the pulse in her neck. After a moment, he sighed and straightened up. She heard him retreating and let herself relax a little, waiting for the sound of the door closing. It didn't come!

Nancy willed herself not to move, but finally she could stand the suspense no longer. Slowly, she shifted her head away from the door and lifted her shoulder enough so she could ease the blindfold above her eyes. Then she turned to the door again.

Oh, no! she thought, when she realized it was wide open, spilling light into the cargo area. Beyond the doorway she could see the passenger cabin. A man was sprawled on one of the seats, his back to her, but close enough to hear if she got up or if Elena came out of hiding again.

Nancy closed her eyes. It was too late to formulate a plan with the Spanish girl. All she could do was lie still and hope that she'd be able to escape when they landed. She dozed as the boring hours crept by.

Finally, the change in the sound of the engines brought Nancy to full awareness. When she opened her eyes, she saw that the man was gone from the passenger area, though the door was still open.

"Nancy?" Elena whispered softly.

"I'm here," the girl detective answered, removing the painful gag and sitting up to massage her aching arms.

"We're landing," Elena said from her hiding place. "What are you going to do?"

Nancy sighed. "I don't know," she admitted. "What about you?"

"I'll try to stay hidden," Elena replied. "If I can sneak away later without being seen, maybe I can find out what is going on before they discover that I'm not in Arizona."

"What should I do?"

"Try to get away from them and hide near the landing strip. I'll find you after I get off. If you can't escape, I'll tell Ricardo what happened and maybe we can find a way to help you. I'm sure the men are not planning to take you anywhere else tonight."

The plane began to descend, and Nancy stood up, leaving her blindfold and gag on the floor. She took her shoulder bag, which had been put beside her, then located the hatch in the side of the plane. After a moment's hesitation, she slipped behind a nearby canvas-covered mount that felt like a piece of heavy farm equipment. When the cargo hatch was opened, she would jump and make a run for it.

A moment later the plane landed roughly. The sound of footsteps could be heard in the passenger cabin after the engines were shut down. "I'll get the girl," her kidnapper declared in Spanish.

"We'll have to . . . " another man said. He came through the connecting door, then stopped suddenly. When Nancy peeked out from under the tarp, she recognized him as the tall, dark man who had followed her in California. "Where is she?" he began, then shouted angrily as the cargo hatch opened wide.

38

Nancy leaped through it onto the hard, grass-covered ground of the runway several feet below her. She rolled over twice, then got up quickly and ran.

It was night, as she had expected. Torches burned along the edge of the runway, marking it clearly, but shedding little illumination on anything else. Nancy heard shouts from the plane and dived between the two nearest torches, crashing into the brush behind. Tree branches and thorns ripped her skin, and the rocks under her feet made her slip and stumble.

"Get her! Get her!" she heard the men cry. Panting, she raced on. After a while, the shouts grew dimmer, and when she looked back, she could not even see the light of the torches. Suddenly she tripped over something. She pitched forward, hitting her head on a sharp object. Nancy gasped in pain, then was enveloped by darkness.

When she regained consciousness, she lay still until her mind began to function again. Her eyes still closed, she vaguely remembered what happened and began to feel around her. Suddenly she touched something furry and warm. The girl sat up abruptly, her hands flying to her head as she did. The throbbing was almost unbearable, and her fingers found a sore lump just above her left temple.

She opened her eyes and stared into the huge green eyes of a sleek black cat.

"Meow!" the cat said, rubbing against Nancy's side. Then he stretched out on the bed next to her.

"Hi, cat," Nancy murmured. "Where am I?"

In the light of a flickering candle, she could see that she was in a large, comfortable bedroom with old, Spanish-style furniture. The musty smell told her that the room had not been used for some time.

Nancy got to her feet and tiptoed to the nearest door, turning the knob cautiously. The door didn't budge.

A second door led to a closet, which contained some clothing, and a third to a small bath. The only window in the room opened onto a balcony overlooking what appeared to be a sheer cliff. Since it was dark outside, Nancy could not tell how far the drop was or what lay below.

She sighed and turned to the cat. "I don't suppose you could tell me how I got here."

He yawned again and settled himself more comfortably on the pillow.

Nancy sat down beside him, then noticed that there was a tray on the bedside table. Curious, she lifted the cover and felt almost weak with hunger from the aroma that rose from the food underneath it. For the first time, she realized that she hadn't eaten since breakfast.

"Well, I don't know who brought me here, but I sure am grateful for this," Nancy observed, feeling silly to be talking to the cat. Yet, the sound of her own voice made her feel less lonely.

The food tasted wonderful, and the small jug of hot chocolate on the tray soothed her sore mouth and throat. It helped her forget the long hours she had spent with the gag in her mouth.

As her strength returned, Nancy also felt less confused and frightened. She stood up, looking at her torn, dirty suit. Her wild escape through the brush had nearly ruined it, and now the cold evening air in the room made her shiver.

"I sure could use a change of clothing," she said to herself, and went to check the closet. With a cry of joy, she found a heavy sweater and jeans her size, as well as a pair of sneakers. She took them out and laid them on the bed.

I'd better take a shower before I put these on, she mused, and went into the bathroom. The water was only tepid, but refreshing, even though it burned the scratches on her skin. After she had dried herself, she found a bottle of soothing lotion and applied the pink liquid freely all over her body.

For a prison, the facilities aren't bad, she thought wryly as she returned to the bedroom and put on her new outfit. Then she combed her wind-tangled hair and looked in the mirror.

"Okay, Nancy," she said to herself. "Hot food and clean clothes are nice, but it's time you found a way to escape." She turned to the bed. "Cat, how do you feel about getting away?" she asked. "Maybe you know a secret exit somewhere?"

Suddenly, she realized that she had been talking to an empty pillow. Her eyes swept around the room, searching for the friendly animal. Then she looked under the bed and behind the furniture. She peered into the bathroom, but there was no sign of the cat anywhere. "Kitty?" she murmured. "Kitty, where are you?"

There was only silence. Nancy put her suit on the bed, then took a nail file from her purse, ready to try the door again. All at once she stopped in her tracks, her eyes on the bedside table. Not only had the emerald-eyed cat disappeared, but so had the tray. Someone had been in her room while she was changing!

Nancy raced to the door, which now opened at her touch. Cautiously she peered into a dark, empty hall, then almost screamed as a shadow moved toward her!

6

Locked In

"Meow," the emerald-eyed cat said, stopping in front of the young detective.

"You scared me half to death," Nancy whispered, then stooped to stroke his sleek black fur. "Who let you out?"

The cat regarded her for a moment, then turned and walked along the hall, his stride purposeful and unhurried. Nancy took a deep breath, picked up the candle and her purse, slipped the book of matches into her pocket, and followed him. He led her to a cobweb-festooned staircase, then vanished before she reached the shadowy lower level.

"Cat, where did you go?" Nancy asked, keeping her voice low, suddenly not sure that she was alone in the echoing corridors of the spooky old house. There was no answering meow and no stir in the shadows but after a moment, Nancy's ears did catch the distant sound of music. She followed the soft notes along the hallway, shielding her flickering flame as the wayward draft teased it.

The music was louder when she reached a bend in the corridor. Nancy hesitated a moment before peering cautiously around the corner. What she saw surprised her. The wide hallway continued in darkness, but it was blocked by a beautiful, floor-to-ceiling, wrought iron grill.

"I'm trapped!" she murmured, shaking the grill and finding that the fancifully-shaped flowers and leaves were strong and immovable. "Now what do I do?"

The music had ended and there was nothing but darkness around her. She retraced her steps to the floor above, which was also closed off by an iron grill beyond the staircase. Nancy tried the doors along the way. All were locked but one, which opened into a windowless library with floor-to-ceiling shelves on all four walls, filled with books, most of them in Spanish.

"Another dead end," Nancy murmured, and returned to her room. I'm in an unused wing of a strange house with no way out, she thought.

What am I going to do?

Wearily, she dropped onto the bed and closed her eyes. "Maybe I can pick the lock to one of the doors tomorrow and find a window that looks out over something else but this cliff!" she murmured to herself.

The long hours of anxiety weighed heavily on her, and soon she was dozing. Suddenly, she heard a faint click. She sat up, her heart pounding, as the door opened, and Elena stepped in.

"Nancy?" she whispered. "Thank goodness you're all right."

Nancy felt a flood of relief, then doubt overshadowed her joy. What if Elena was one of her kidnappers? After all, the plane that had brought her here belonged to Elena's family, and now the girl seemed to be her jailer.

"How did I get here?" Nancy asked.

Elena sank into a chair. "Ricardo carried you. I managed to get off the plane without being seen." She smiled. "Everyone was very busy chasing you. I met Ricardo and told him you needed help. He led the others away, then we looked for you. We found you lying on the ground next to one of our tractors. Apparently you hit your head on it. We brought you here, hoping you'd be safe in the old wing of the hacienda."

Nancy felt the bruise on her head and

grimaced. "Buy why am I locked in?" she asked.

"For your own protection," Elena explained. "I don't think anyone but my cat Maro comes here. I was going to explain earlier, but you were in the shower and I had to get back to Ricardo. I just wanted to make sure those men didn't find you."

Nancy stiffened. "Do you believe there's a chance they will come here looking for me?" she asked, remembering the terror of her flight into the brush.

"I don't think so now, but we didn't know at first."

"What do you mean?"

"Well, they stopped searching after you disappeared into the brush. They unloaded the equipment, put it on a truck, and left for another part of the estate. As far as I've been able to determine, no one in the house is looking for you, Nancy." Elena pushed back her long, black hair.

Nancy met the dark eyes and knew deep down that Elena was her friend. She decided to trust the girl completely. She told her what had happened in Phoenix and San Pedro, then asked, "Do you know of any connection between your family and the three freighters that sank near Cartagena a few months ago?" she asked.

46

Elena shook her head. "I don't think my family owns ships. Of course, I don't know that much about the business. I used to, but I've been away at college and this time, when I came home for vacation, Aunt Rosalinda, as I mentioned before, didn't bring me up to date. I never dreamed that something like this could happen to us."

"Could she be having a breakdown of some sort?" Nancy asked.

"I don't know. It's a mystery to me. I—" Elena suddenly brightened. "Nancy, you told me you were a detective. Maybe *you* could solve this mystery!"

"I'd like to," Nancy said. "But to do that, I have to get away from here. Besides, I have to contact my father. He has no idea what has happened to me and he must be frantic with worry by now."

Elena nodded. "I understand. That should be your first priority. But why do you want to leave? Obviously your case and my mystery are somehow connected, or you wouldn't have been brought here. Nancy, the solution to your investigation may be right here at the del Luz hacienda!"

"I know that," Nancy said. "But I can't do any investigating while I'm a captive in this place and unable to move about freely."

"I understand," Elena said. "We have to—"

The sound of approaching footsteps interrupted her sentence. Nancy leaped to her feet, but before she could move any farther, the door burst open and a tall, handsome young man came in. He had black, curly hair and an open, attractive face. A charming grin softened his rather grave expression as he looked at Nancy.

"I am Ricardo," he said in heavily-accented English. "Please excuse me for breaking in this way, but it is a matter of urgency." He turned to Elena. "I believe we can visit your aunt without being seen, if we do it immediately," he told her.

"Then we must go," Elena said urgently, leaping to her feet. "Forgive me, Nancy. Ricardo and I will talk with you later, but we have to go to Aunt Rosalinda now."

Before Nancy could ask any questions, the two had left the room and were racing down the corridor.

Nancy hesitated for a moment, then started after them. But by the time she reached the top of the staircase, they'd vanished, leaving only silence and darkness in their wake. The grills were in place and securely locked. Nancy was still a prisoner, and as she returned wearily to her room, her only companion was Maro, the black cat.

Angry, exhausted, and more than a little frightened, the girl detective lay down on the musty bed. As she closed her eyes, she wondered if she'd ever be able to escape from the hacienda!

A light touch caressed Nancy's cheek. She sighed and stirred. It touched her again, and this time she realized that it was Maro's furry paw. She opened her eyes and gazed at the cat.

"Good morning," she murmured, seeing sunlight streaming in through the window. Her head still hurt a little as she sat up and looked around. Her room appeared exactly as it had when she went to sleep. There was no sign that Elena had returned during the night.

"Too bad we can't call room service," Nancy told Maro when she got to her feet and stretched her stiff muscles. Her stomach rumbled with hunger as she washed, combed her hair, and put on fresh lipstick. Maro was still on the bed when she stepped out of the bathroom. Nancy tried the door and found it unlocked.

Frustrated and hungry, she wandered out into the hall. In the daylight, she could appreciate the impressive Spanish architecture of the place, which, despite its beauty, had a forbidding atmosphere. Cobwebs linked every bar and curlique of the decor, and dust lay like gray fur on the dark metal of the grill that barred her way.

"This hasn't been opened for years," Nancy observed to the cat, who was padding along behind her. "How did Elena and Ricardo get into this part of the house?"

Maro stretched, yawned, then slipped through the bars of the grill, disappearing into the dark hall beyond.

"Thanks a lot, cat," Nancy murmured, staring after the sleek animal. Then she went downstairs. Again, all she found were locked rooms and a grill just beneath the one on the second floor. She retraced her steps and saw another flight of stairs leading to a third story. She had no better luck there. More locked rooms, another grill. When she walked back to the stairs, she noted that her footsteps were the only ones visible in the dust. No one has been up here in ages, Nancy deduced. She went downstairs again, examining the floor closely. On the second floor she could see many footprints, some large, some smaller. She suddenly realized that they led into the library she had briefly inspected the previous night.

She followed the tracks into the book-filled room and paused. She surveyed the floor carefully, then continued along the trail of footprints to a section of the bookcases near the ornate stone fireplace that dominated one wall.

"Aha," the girl said softly, noticing the smudged shelf. "You're not going to keep me a prisoner in this wing for long, Elena. Not if I can figure out how this panel works . . ."

7

A Secret Passage

Deftly Nancy's fingers examined the wood until she heard a click. She jumped back, startled. A section of the shelves swung soundlessly open! Beyond was a narrow stone ledge and steps leading down into the darkness.

Nancy hurried back into her room to get the pencil flashlight she always carried in her pocketbook. When she could not find it, she sighed.

I must have lost it, she thought, and grabbed the candle and matchbook instead. Moments later she was descending the stairwell behind the bookcase. The air was damp and cold, and its shifting currents made her candle flicker erractically. The steps were narrow and worn, and the young detective was glad when she reached the bottom. She found herself in a passage that seemed to wind through the very walls of the old mansion.

"I don't blame Maro for taking the other route," she murmured as she passed a dark opening. "This place is like a cave."

Her voice echoed spookily, making her even more conscious of being alone. She was glad to find another set of stone steps just past the opening of a second side passage. Cautiously, she climbed up, shielding her dancing candle flame.

The steps ended in a ledge similar to the one she'd found beyond the bookcase in the library. A small handle was set in the old wood of the wall. Nancy waited, chewing nervously on her lower lip. She was eager to escape, but she was not anxious to fall into the hands of the men who'd kidnapped her in Phoenix.

Placing her ear against the wood, she listened. There was no sound from beyond. She took a deep breath, grasped the handle, and turned it. The panel opened with a faint click, and she found herself in what appeared to be a closet. Light filtered in from a partly-open door on the far side of a neat row of coats and jackets that hung there.

Relieved, Nancy blew out her candle, closed the panel, and stepped forward. Carefully, she peered out the door.

"Wow!" The word slipped out as she stared at a new world. Beautiful Spanish tile gleamed beneath her feet, and ornately-carved benches and chairs stood in what appeared to be the foyer of the hacienda. Nancy made sure she was alone, then stepped out into the sunny room.

There was a closed door on one side, a beautiful parlor on the other. The closet itself was under a grand staircase that ascended from the foyer to the second floor. In front of her, a wide corridor led to the rear of the mansion. Nancy hesitated. Then her sensitive nose caught the faint aroma of food, and her stomach rumbled in response.

She followed the scent along the corridor, passing an open dining room that could comfortably seat thirty people, then peeked through a swinging door into a shiny, modern kitchen. It was empty.

Several dishes stood on one of the counters— the source of the delicious aromas. They contained sausage, eggs, several kinds of sweet rolls, and toast.

Hungrily, Nancy took a plate from the stack on a nearby shelf and helped herself to several sausages, eggs, and toast. Then she wrapped four sweet rolls in a napkin for future rations. Aware of her vulnerability, she retreated to the closet, hiding herself in its peaceful dimness while she devoured the feast.

Eating restored her spirits and bolstered her determination to investigate the mansion. When she had finished, she left her plate on a shelf and let herself back into the foyer. It still appeared deserted as she went up the stairs to the second floor.

A long hall flanked on both sides by doors led toward the rear of the building. Nancy followed it and cautiously opened each door, peering into several bedrooms. There was no sign of neglect, but none of the rooms was occupied.

When Nancy opened the last door on the right-hand side, it banged slightly against a small footstool behind it. The next moment, Nancy stared into the startled eyes of an elderly woman resting in bed.

"Mariposa, you have come back!" The woman's voice was high and shrill, and the words were in Spanish.

Nancy stood still, too shocked to move.

"Come in, Mariposa, please. I missed you so much." The speaker's face was pale and lined, and her dark eyes were shadowed, as though she'd suffered greatly. Her black hair was liberally threaded with silver. It curled softly around her face, and Nancy could see that she'd once been a great beauty.

"I'm sorry I walked in on you," Nancy began, convinced the woman was Rosalinda del Luz. "I was looking for Elena."

"Elena is at school, you know that," the woman answered. "But please, come closer. You do not look any older than you were the day you left to marry Paolo. Where have you been so long? Why did you let me think you were dead?" Her dark eyes were feverish, and the hands that reached out to her were thin and delicate.

"My name is Nancy Drew," the girl whispered as she closed the door behind her.

"Mariposa, do not tease me," the woman cried. "I have been ill, and they are trying to trick me. I need your help now, little sister. It is why you have come back—to help me?" The frail body moved nervously under the silken bedcovers. Nancy could sense the woman's agitation, and it frightened her.

"I'm sorry," she said. "Of course I'll help you. What can I do? Who is trying to trick you?"

Rosalinda del Luz settled back in the old-fashioned, draped canopy bed, and a warm smile lit up her delicate features. "It is so good to have you here. Elena has deserted me. I tried to be a mother to her, just as I knew you would want me to, but I never see her and they say she has changed."

"Who says so?" Nancy asked, hating to pretend to be someone she wasn't, yet afraid to argue with the old woman.

"Señor Cordova does. He says that he will take care of everything for me, but I am not sure I trust him, Mariposa. He seems kind and competent, but there is something . . . Will you take care of things for a while, little sister? I need to rest and not have the bad dreams. I need someone . . . " A thin hand reached out and grasped Nancy's warm fingers with surprising strength.

"I'm here," Nancy soothed. "I'll help, if you'll just tell me what you want me to do."

"Have you seen the cat?" Rosalinda's eyes were suddenly wary.

"The cat?" The abrupt change of subject left Nancy confused.

"The emerald-eyed cat, have you seen it? Is it safe? We cannot let them get it."

"I saw him just a little while ago," Nancy assured her. "He was fine."

Rosalinda's anguish faded. "Take care of the cat," she whispered. "It is all that is left."

"I don't understand," Nancy protested, but the tight grip was already loosening, and the woman slumped back against her pillows, her eyes closed.

8

Danger in the Hall

For a moment, Nancy thought the woman had fainted, then a soft snore rippled through the air. Rosalinda del Luz was asleep.

Nancy watched her for several minutes, hoping she would awaken and explain her statements. However, the woman seemed exhausted, and Nancy rose with a sigh to explore the room for some clue to the source of Rosalinda's problem.

There was a collection of photographs on the mantelpiece, and when Nancy looked at them, she gasped in surprise. A large picture, faded now, showed two young women. One was Rosalinda, the other, a reddish-blond girl who bore a striking resemblance to Nancy.

Mariposa! the young detective thought. No wonder Rosalinda was surprised to find me in

58

her room. She stepped back from the fireplace and noticed an elegant drape hanging behind the collection of pictures. Curious, she tugged at the corded pull, then gasped when she saw the painting that the drapery had covered.

It was a study of Rosalinda and Mariposa, again as young girls. But what drew Nancy's attention was the large glass case that separated the two and formed the focal point of the portrait. It held art objects of great beauty—a silver unicorn with a ruby collar, a golden rabbit, a tiny golden crown set with jewels, and a cat with green eyes.

"So that's what Rosalinda was talking about," Nancy murmured as she admired the largest of the treasures. The animal was life-sized with flashing emerald eyes and a magnificent collar of diamonds.

Nancy glanced at the sleeping woman, wanting to wake her and ask her questions. But she was aware that Rosalinda's mental state was too precarious for conclusive answers. Swallowing a sigh, she closed the drape over the portrait.

Rosalinda del Luz whimpered and shifted a little, settling deeper into her sleep. Nancy touched her hand gently. "I'll be back," she whispered, "and I will try to help, I promise."

The hall appeared deserted when she left the woman's room and started back toward the front of the house. Her mind was on Elena now that she'd seen the condition of her aunt. Where were the girl and her fiance?

Suddenly Nancy heard a woman's voice nearby.

" . . . but, Señor, I cannot do more than I have," the stranger said in Spanish.

Nancy skidded to a halt and looked around wildly. For a moment she thought of retreating to Rosalinda's room, but before she could move, there was the click of a door opening just ahead of her.

Nancy saw an alcove a few steps away and raced to it on her toes, trying not to make a sound as she slipped into the shadowy recess, frantically seeking a hiding place. There was little choice—a small plant stand and a fragile chair were the only pieces of furniture, and neither would conceal her very well.

"We cannot afford to wait much longer," a man said. "I have given too much time to this project already, and I must be able to reap the benefits of my hard work."

Nancy searched desperately for a way to disappear. Her eyes focused on the huge tapestry that covered the rear wall of the alcove. It hung to the floor and in the half-light, half-shadow of the area, it did offer some hope. She squeezed past the chair and lifted the heavy fabric, trying to slide behind it without pulling it from the wall.

"She could be permanently damaged if we go too far," the woman was saying as the two came closer, then seemed to stop directly outside the alcove. "Elena has become suspicious. There was talk before she went back to school."

"Do not trouble yourself about that one or her nosy young man; they will not bother us for a while. We must get the old woman's signature, then we can safely put her in a home and go on with our plans for the future."

The man sounded so threatening that Nancy instinctively retreated farther back behind the tapestry, afraid that he might notice the telltale bulge she made in the thick, dusty fabric. As she did, her heel got caught in the ragged fringe at the bottom of the wall hanging.

Terrified of bringing down her frail hiding place, Nancy reached behind her, digging her fingernails into the wall to keep her balance. Her hands closed over something that stuck out from the smooth wooden surface, and a click echoed in her ear, the next instant, the wall moved, and she tumbled backwards into darkness.

Rolling herself into a ball, Nancy lay still, sure that she would be discovered. The click sounded again, loud and clear in the thick silence.

"What was that?" the man asked, his voice muffled now.

"I do not know," the woman answered. "It came from the alcove."

"I hope Rosalinda has not taken to prowling about the house again," the man grumbled.

"She is too weak," the woman assured him. "I have seen to that."

"Well, it had to be something." The man's voice was ominously close to Nancy.

She fought an almost irresistible urge to sneeze as the dust swirled around her. Though her eyes were wide open, she could see nothing in the blackness, and she dared not move.

Suddenly the woman's laugh filled the air. "It was the cat," she said. "Maro, you black beast, what are you doing up here? Have you not learned yet that this house is not yours now that your friend Elena is gone?"

The cat growled.

"We will get rid of that creature, too, as soon as everything is signed and ready to go, Isabella," the man said.

"Si, Señor Cordova. It cannot be too soon for me," Isabella answered. "I do not enjoy my work any longer."

Your work, Nancy thought. I wonder what it all entails.

The two started to move away, and Nancy let her breath out slowly, her whole body shaking with the tension caused by her close call. She was safe from discovery for the moment, she realized. *But where was she?*

She'd stumbled through another secret panel, one hidden by the tapestry. Beyond that, she had no idea whether she'd fallen on a ledge above another stone stairway, or if she was in a level passage. She was almost afraid to move.

She realized that Señor Cordova was the man who was running the huge estate, but who was Isabella? And what had they done to Rosalinda del Luz?

Nancy eased herself into a sitting position, exploring the area around her with her fingers as these questions raced through her mind. And what had Cordova meant when he said they didn't need to worry about Elena and Ricardo? What had he done to them?

An icy chill ran down the girl's spine as she realized just how alone she would be without her friends, and she shuddered. What if she was trapped forever in this blackness? What if she couldn't find a way out?

9

Hidden Treasure

Nancy fought back a wave of panic. She couldn't give in to fear now; she had to escape and find out what had happened to Elena and Ricardo. She also needed to help Rosalinda del Luz and protect her from whatever evil plot Señor Cordova and Isabella were trying to carry out.

Matches, she thought, suddenly remembering that she'd put them in her pocket before leaving the old wing. It took her only a moment to light one.

She was in a small, crowded room. A candle stood on a table near the panel she'd tumbled through. She lit it before the match burned her fingers. The glow revealed something that made her heart leap with excitement.

"Oh!" Nancy suppressed a squeal of joy. The flickering light was reflected by the glass case she had seen in the painting, and the case contained one of the lovely figures, the emerald-eyed cat!

The girl detective opened the case with shaking hands and lifted the treasure out, surprised by its heavy weight. Her fingers traced the exquisite diamond collar. The gold and gems alone must be worth a fortune, she thought, yet the delicate workmanship makes the piece more valuable still as an art object.

"I wonder what happened to your friends, cat," she murmured, thinking of the unicorn and the rabbit she had seen in the portrait. Then, with a sigh, she replaced the cat in the case and turned her attention to the rest of the room.

There were a number of boxes and trunks stacked haphazardly around the small table. Nancy checked them quickly, but found nothing similar to the golden cat. There were plenty of old books, papers, some clothing, and photographs, but nothing that offered any answers to what was going on at the troubled hacienda.

Eager to find Elena and Ricardo, Nancy turned her attention to the panel again. She located the handle that opened it from the inside, and slipped out of the secret room, staying behind the tapestry until she was sure there was no one nearby. Then she cautiously advanced into the hall.

She wondered if she should return to Rosalinda's room and try to talk to her once more, but the woman's confusion and frailty discouraged her.

That left Elena and Ricardo. Nancy decided to retreat to the unused part of the house. If they were still free, they would look for her there.

She tiptoed along the upper hall, pausing frequently to listen and watch for anyone who might be coming. The house seemed empty, and after only a moment of hesitation, she started down the stairs. She'd just reached the bottom when a door across the foyer opened, revealing what appeared to be an office.

Nancy froze, trapped in the open with nowhere to hide. A stocky, dark-haired man stood in the doorway, his black eyes meeting her startled gaze.

"Hello, there, young lady, may I help you?" The words were spoken in fluent English and the smile was pleasant, but the voice was that of the man she had overheard outside the alcove! He was Señor Cordova!

She took a step backward, stumbling on the stairs.

"Where are you going?" His tone was cold and threatening now.

Nancy whirled around and raced up the stairs and along the hall to the rear of the building. She came to a second stairway leading to the third floor, and took the steps two at a time. The man shouted for her to stop, but she ran until she found a small closet to hide in.

Time passed. Her breathing finally slowed and she strained her ears, expecting a search, but none came! Cordova hadn't even chased her, Nancy realized with a chill; he was so sure that she was trapped in the house that he didn't feel the need to lock her up.

Confused and very much alone, the young detective finally emerged from the closet and retraced her steps to her room in the old wing. Just as she'd feared, there was no sign that Elena or Ricardo had come back. Discouraged and weary, Nancy ate the rolls from her purse and pondered what to do next.

She went to the window and looked out over the empty countryside that stretched away from the base of the cliff. Her search of the house so far had revealed no telephone that she could use to reach her father. But there must be a way to communicate with the rest of the world from here, the girl thought—maybe from somewhere outside the house.

"Meow!" Nancy turned to see her door opening as the black cat pushed his way in.

"Well, Maro, I'm happy to see you," she told him, dropping to her knees and stroking the cat's sleek fur. "You did me a good turn in the hall today."

The cat's purr increased in volume as he rippled under her fingers. "Now, if you could just tell me how to get out of here . . . " Nancy's voice trailed off as Maro leaped onto the bed and kneaded himself a nest in the covers. He settled down with a yawn that revealed sharp white teeth, then his green eyes closed.

"Thanks, anyway," Nancy told him. "I'll try on my own. There must be a way out, because I'm sure Ricardo didn't carry me in through the front door with Señor Cordova watching."

She recalled the side tunnels she'd noticed on her two trips through the secret passage. I'd better check them out, she decided, and went to the library. Once again she descended the stone stairs. The first passage proved to be a dead end, terminated by a pile of fallen rock, but the second rose steeply to a small door.

Nancy hesitated, afraid of what she might find on the other side. Then she took a deep breath and turned the ornate, old handle. To her surprise and relief, the door opened soundlessly into a thick tangle of green vines!

"Ricardo and Elena must have come in this way," she thought, noting that several of the vines were withered and broken. "Now if I only knew where they are!"

The outside world was bright with sunlight. What had once been beautiful, formal gardens stretched in every direction, but the signs of neglect were obvious. Weeds and grass choked the flowerbeds, and trees and bushes grew in wild profusion, untrimmed and uncared for. In the distance, the property was surrounded by a tall stone wall. A guard was walking along the road near the gate.

"It's a fortress," Nancy mused. "No wonder Señor Cordova is so sure I can't escape!"

She moved through the heavy undergrowth circling the huge building. The opposite side overlooked the cliff she'd seen from her window. In the rear, there were a stable, three sheds, and a fenced-in area where a number of burros were grazing.

Following an overgrown section of citrus trees, Nancy made her way to the compound. The curious animals trotted toward her immediately. Their leader, a dainty white jenny, extended her nose over the rail to sniff at Nancy's arm.

"Hello there," the girl said, patting the velvety nose, then scratching behind the long ears. "You're a friendly creature."

The rest of the burros wheeled and moved away at the sound of her voice, but the white jenny stayed, following Nancy along the fence as she headed for the stable. It was the first place she planned to search, and a moment later she slipped into the shadow of the small building.

It was empty. The stalls were not in use, and the hay was musty and dry. Elena and Ricardo were not there, so Nancy moved on, investigating the sheds, searching among farm equipment, seed, and old riding tack. But there was no sign of her friends.

Where can they be? Nancy asked herself, leaning against the outer wall of the last shed, her frustration and worry bringing her close to tears. She felt helpless with the huge mansion looming above her, knowing that guards patrolled the outer perimeters of the grounds.

A shout interrupted her thoughts, and Nancy looked around, afraid that she'd been spotted. Señor Cordova had emerged from the rear of the house and was striding rapidly in her direction. The girl detective dropped to her knees and scuttled backward into a thick tangle of flowering bushes.

There were sounds of running feet, and in a moment she saw several men coming close to her hiding place. Her blood chilled as she realized that Señor Cordova had called in his guards. Obviously, he wanted them to search for her.

"There is an American girl on the property," he began, his rapid Spanish rather difficult for Nancy to follow. "I want her found and taken to Mesa del Oro to join the others." He described Nancy carefully, finishing, "She must not be allowed to leave the estate grounds. Is that clear? No matter what, she must not escape!"

The men murmured in assent and hurried back to their posts. Nancy cowered beneath the protective branches of the sheltering bush, watching Señor Cordova survey the area with cold eyes, his face hard and ugly.

She shivered, realizing what his words meant. He wanted her sent to wherever he was holding Elena and Ricardo!

10

Escape

Once Cordova had returned to the house, Nancy began her long and dangerous retreat to the hidden door. It was clear to her now that escaping from the estate would be almost impossible. Moreover, since she had no idea where the hacienda was located, she would not know where to go even if she could get outside the walls.

Alone in her musty room, Nancy lay down beside Maro, stroking the cat and trying to think. The outbuildings had revealed no clue, but the conversation she'd overheard had told her where Elena and Ricardo were being held—if indeed they were the "others" that Cordova had referred to. But where was Mesa del Oro?

"Well, I can't just hide here with you forever, Maro," she finally told the cat. "I have to help Elena, Ricardo, and Señora Rosalinda."

The cat began to purr loudly.

"There has to be a phone somewhere," Nancy mused. "Maybe in that office. If I could get in there and call Dad . . ."

The idea quickly became a plan. She would wait until very late at night, then slip out of her room and go to the office, call her father, and search for a clue to why she'd been kidnapped.

Though hunger made her restless, Nancy waited until well after midnight, unwilling to risk being caught. The house was silent when she let herself out of the closet into the foyer. Moonlight shone in through the windows, making it easier for her to see. Though she longed to raid the refrigerator, she went resolutely toward the office.

The knob turned easily under her touch, but the door didn't budge. Oh, no, she thought. He keeps it locked!

She set to work with her nail file, and in a moment the tumblers clicked and the door swung open. With her heart pounding, she hurried in and looked for a telephone. There was none!

Sighing, Nancy set her candle on the desk. "Well, let's see what he *does* keep in here," she murmured, opening the desk drawers and beginning a systematic search of the records.

Her disappointment over the missing telephone was quickly forgotten as she made discovery after discovery. Financial statements told her that the hacienda was the nerve center for a huge estate with holdings all over the world. They seemed to cover a vast variety of enterprises.

Nancy also found two important documents. One was the Last Will and Testament of Carlos del Luz, in which he left control of the estate to his wife, Rosalinda, and to his niece, Elena Escobar, on the day she became twenty-one. The other was an unsigned Power of Attorney made out to Señor Cordova.

"So that's why time is running out," Nancy murmured. "Elena will be twenty-one soon. She'll marry Ricardo and they won't need Cordova. That's why he's trying to force Rosalinda into signing the Power of Attorney."

Another file showed that Isabella, the housekeeper, had been hired by Señor Cordova a few days after Elena had left for college. This made Nancy suspect that she'd been employed to help Cordova change the independent aunt whom Elena had loved into the terrified stranger Nancy had talked to so briefly.

The young detective sighed, replacing the

papers. She'd solved the mystery, but it gave her no satisfaction, since she had no idea how she could use the information to help Elena or her aunt. Frustrated, she looked around the room.

Her eyes fell on a wall hanging above the file cabinets. She lifted the candle for closer inspection and realized that it was an old map of the estate.

Some of the drawing was faded and the lettering was in Spanish, but after a few minutes, Nancy was able to locate the burro pasture, which turned out to be much larger than she had realized, and, beyond it, a road. The village of Mesa del Oro was not too far south from there!

Tingling with excitement, Nancy looked for a piece of paper and a pen so she could copy that section of the huge map. As she turned, her elbow hit the heavy, brass desk lamp and pushed it to one side. She grabbed the lamp to keep it from falling, but she wasn't quick enough to catch an ornate box that stood on the other side. It crashed to the floor, popping open to reveal a telephone!

The noise froze Nancy on the spot. She should run, she knew, yet the lure of the telephone was too great. It was her only chance to get in touch with her father . . .

She dropped to her knees beside the box and picked up the receiver. Before she could dial, however, she heard a door slamming somewhere. Knowing that she hadn't a chance of reaching the closet sanctuary, Nancy blew out her candle and slipped under the desk out of sight.

Nothing happened for a few moments and she began to hope that somehow she'd escaped detection. She reached out for the phone box, planning to strike a match and call the operator.

Just then, however, the office door banged open and the light flashed on, nearly blinding her as she jerked back into her hiding place. She realized, even as she did so, that her candle was still sitting on the desk in plain sight.

"Who is in here?" Isabella demanded.

Nancy held her breath.

"Maro, where are you, you bad cat?" The woman came closer, picked up the telephone box, and set it back on the desk. "If you did this, Señor Cordova will be after your hide."

Isabella's feet were almost close enough for Nancy to touch. A moment later, the girl heard a sharp intake of breath and knew that the woman had seen the candle and realized what it meant.

"You are in here, girl," Isabella said, her tone threatening now as she backed away from the desk. "You cannot hide from me." Nancy looked up and saw the hard face peering at her, the thin-lipped mouth opening to scream. She slipped out of her hiding place, holding out a hand. "Please, Isabella," she began, "I was brought here by kidnappers and I just want to leave. If you'll help me—"

But the woman yelled loudly and grabbed Nancy's arms, twisting them behind the girl's back.

Nancy's training as an athlete enabled her to break the vise-like grip. But as she whirled around, Isabella doubled her fist and moved to strike her. Nancy ducked and thrust out her arms, throwing the woman off balance. Isabella went down in a heap behind the big desk.

Instantly, Nancy grabbed her candle and fled across the foyer into the closet. As she opened the secret panel and stepped through it, she heard the heavy pounding of feet above her and knew that Señor Cordova was on his way!

Nancy lit her candle and hurried down the stone steps into the passage that led to the outside. A plan was forming in her mind. It would take Cordova and Isabella a while to search the house, and she was hoping they wouldn't look beyond it until they were positive that she'd escaped.

In the darkness, it was much easier to make her way around the house. She stopped at the shed where the riding equipment was kept and risked lighting a match to locate a battered halter and lead rope. Then she headed toward the compound, hoping that the white jenny was still as friendly as she had been earlier.

But when she reached the fence, lights suddenly sprung up all along the high wall. Running feet and shouts echoed in the night air! Nancy slipped through the fence quickly, heading for the brush alongside a small ravine that ran through most of the field. There was no sign of the burro herd, but for the moment, she was more concerned with staying hidden than anything else.

The brush caught in her sweater and pulled her hair. Nancy moved ahead cautiously, pausing often to listen for pursuit. At first she heard nothing, but by the time she reached the midpoint of the field, there was a crackling behind her.

Nancy froze, crouching beside a rocky outcropping. The noise continued. It sounded like footsteps of more than one person. Yet no one spoke. Nancy tried to make herself smaller, burying her fair hair and light skin in her dark-clad arms. Suddenly, something touched her back. Nancy leaped to her feet, stifling a scream.

11

Mesa del Oro

The frightened girl stared into the face of the white burro, who jumped back, then looked at her questioningly, its long ears twitching.

"Oh!" Nancy breathed. "You scared me half to death."

The jenny, evidently trusting Nancy, came forward again, her soft muzzle sniffing at the girl's pockets. Nancy scratched her for a moment, then slipped the halter on her.

"You must be someone's pet," she said in relief when the burro accepted the halter without protest and followed her along the ravine. "I just hope you like to be ridden."

When there was a break in the ground cover, Nancy peered back at the mansion. The old house loomed against the night sky, and she could see the guards standing ready on the walls. Lights illuminated all approaches to the gates.

Will they think of looking this way? Nancy wondered. Or are they sure she couldn't have escaped through the pasture? She tried to remember the details on the map in Cordova's office, but she had had little time to study it, and the candle's light had been unsteady.

The terrain began to change, and suddenly Nancy found herself in a thicket of trees that continued endlessly. At first she was relieved, for she felt safer in the shelter of the spreading branches. But then she began to worry about getting lost.

"Little burro, do you know where we're going?" she asked.

The white head rubbed against her arm as the creature moved along next to her without hesitation. Nancy rested an arm across the animal's furry withers, allowing herself to be led through the forest.

Suddenly several dark shapes materialized around them. After her initial fright, Nancy realized she was surrounded by the entire burro herd! They all made their way along purposefully, not halting until they topped a small rise, and a break in the trees showed the fence at the end of the compound.

Nancy swallowed hard. The road she'd seen on the map was nowhere to be seen!

"Now how do I find Mesa del Oro?" she asked herself, staring at the forest on the far side of the fence.

There was no gate, but the fence was built of small logs resting on notched posts, and Nancy could simply lift two logs and lead the white burro through. When the rest followed, Nancy felt a twinge of guilt, then she smiled.

"Maybe Cordova will think you broke out on your own," she giggled. "I just hope we're not escaping into total wilderness, where we'll all starve to death."

The burros spread out to graze in a thick carpet of grass beneath the trees. Nancy watched them for a moment, then sighed. "Well, where *some of us* will starve to death," she amended.

She led her jenny forward a short distance, seeking a clearing in the forest, then looked up at the stars, trying to remember the constellations that would be overhead in this part of the world. The intense darkness of the night made the stars wonderfully visible. It took her only a few moments to establish her directions. South should be this way, she decided, pointing left. Maybe if I go straight for a little longer, I'll get to the road after all.

Nancy spotted a distant rise and started toward it, still leading the jenny, not wanting to ride her until she was more confident of where they were going. The other burros watched their departure. Only one followed, and it stopped to graze again after only a few steps.

"They don't have much confidence in my sense of direction, do they?" Nancy asked, feeling much the same way.

The hike through the dark forest seemed endless, and she was beginning to lose hope. Suddenly, the burro stopped, her ears bent sharply forward as though she was expecting something. Nancy took a stronger hold on the lead rope and held her breath, not sure what they might be facing. The sounds of a motor could be heard almost at once, then they stopped as light beams penetrated the brush just ahead of her.

"Do you really think she could make it this far?" a man asked in Spanish.

"I did not think she could even get away from the hacienda," Señor Cordova growled.

The burro stamped her small hooves and lifted her head, but the young detective clamped strong fingers over her muzzle before she could bray and give their position away. It was obvious that the jenny shared Nancy's feelings about Señor Cordova. However, this was not the time to express them.

"Where would she be heading?" the other man asked.

"Away from the hacienda," was the answer, "and that is the one thing we cannot risk. She must be caught and held until— We just do not want her wandering around loose." Señor Cordova finished, obviously not trusting his companion with his plans.

"Shall we patrol the roads?" the man asked.

"We will have to if Isabella has not found her when we get back to the house," Señor Cordova replied. "Now let us go and see if anyone else has been more successful."

The motor roared, the car turned around, and after a moment the lights disappeared. Nancy let out her breath in relief, then patted the burro, who was nibbling the grass at her feet.

"Well, I guess we're on our way now," the girl said. "How do you feel about being ridden?" She vaulted onto the small creature's back, feeling oversized, since her feet hung close to the ground. The animal looked at her for a moment, then trotted forward into the open roadway. Nancy didn't even have to guide her as she turned her head south toward Mesa del Oro.

The ride was a nightmare. The road was dusty and winding, and as the burro kept on walking, Nancy had to be continually on the alert, for patrols were soon driving by at irregular intervals. Each time she heard the distant sound of an engine, she had to dismount and lead her burro off the road into the shelter of whatever trees or brush were available. She was in constant fear of being caught in the open by one of the drivers.

Hunger nagged at her, reminding her that lunch had consisted only of sweet rolls, and she'd had no dinner. Toward dawn, exhaustion caught up with her and she found herself dozing as the patient creature trotted along.

"What . . . huh?" Nancy started, nearly falling off the jenny's back.

She blinked in the paling light of dawn, wondering why the animal had stopped. Then she realized that they were standing at the base of a small rise. Above them were the first signs of human habitation. Trees, fences, a few roof peaks and chimneys could be seen, but there was no sign of any people.

"Good girl," Nancy said, patting the tired burro as she slipped off. She nearly fell as her knees buckled. Desperately, she clung to the animal until feeling returned to her legs, then she studied the terrain.

The road led to a village, but to the left was a narrow path winding up a small hill. Nancy tied the burro to a tree, and it began to graze contentedly while the girl crossed the road and scrambled up the rough path. It was a steep climb, but once she reached the top, she was rewarded for her effort. Though there was no signpost on the dusty road, she recognized from the layout of the village that she'd found Mesa del Oro.

Eight small buildings were loosely grouped around an open plaza with a water well. All the houses looked deserted but one.

A battered motor scooter was parked in front of it and an armed guard sat on the porch. Nancy had no doubt that Elena and Ricardo were inside. The question was, how could she get them out?

12

Rescue Attempt

Nancy made her way back to where the white burro waited. She slipped off the halter, then hugged the little creature. "Think you can find your way home, girl?" she asked. "Go rejoin your friends and convince everyone that you had nothing to do with my escape."

The burro nuzzled her for a moment, then turned and trotted into the brush, as though she'd actually understood Nancy's command. The girl stared after the animal for a time, then turned her attention to the village on the mesa above her.

She climbed up the road and began working her way carefully around the rear of the houses, heading for the one where she'd seen the guard.

A glance in the windows of each structure confirmed what she'd suspected. The houses were deserted. Mesa del Oro was a ghost town except for the one building!

When she reached it, Nancy slowed. There was little danger of her being seen from the porch as she moved along the back wall, so she peered in the rear window. What she saw made her gasp. Elena and Ricardo were seated in the room tied to their chairs, gagged. Elena's tear-streaked face was turned her way, and Nancy could see the joy in her friend's eyes as their gazes locked. The young detective waved and held a finger to her lips, even though she knew it was unnecessary.

Nancy sat down on her heels, pondering a plan. Since there was no one in the room with the two captives, she could lure the guard away from the door and slip inside while he was gone. Then she could free Elena and Ricardo, and the three of them would then be able to overpower the jailer.

But how to do it? Nancy retreated to a sheltering bush and studied the area carefully. The most tumble-down of the deserted buildings was on the far side of the well. Nancy felt that it would serve her purpose perfectly. Her decision made, she inched toward it gathering an armload of dry wood, damp leaves and other debris.

"I hope they didn't nail the door and windows shut," she thought when she reached the old shack.

There was no window in the rear of the place, just a yawning opening Nancy could slip through with ease. Once inside, she examined the fireplace and set to work building a fire. It took several minutes to catch properly, then Nancy placed the smoke-producing debris over the crackling flames and retreated.

Her heart pounding, she worked her way back to the building next to the one holding Elena and Ricardo. From there she could see the guard clearly.

Minutes passed, and nothing happened. Nancy chewed her lip, debating another type of diversion but nothing short of burning down one of the buildings was likely to work, unless . . .

Suddenly the guard leaped to his feet, shouting angrily. He looked in both directions, then raced toward the smoking cabin. Nancy hurried into the shadows near the porch, and when the man plunged into the other structure, she raced to the door, praying that it wasn't locked. In a moment, she was inside.

Quickly she jerked the gags off Ricardo and

Elena, then untied their ropes. "Nancy," Elena gasped, "thank God you've come!"

"Speak softly," Nancy whispered. "Your guard is just across the square and may come back at any time. Stay where you are just in case he decides to check on you."

"You are alone?" Ricardo asked.

"Yes. Are you two all right?"

Elena nodded. "We were afraid that they'd caught you," she said. "How did you escape? Is my aunt all right?"

"I'll explain later," Nancy said, and crossed to the front of the cabin, where she peered through the filthy window. What she saw made her heart stop for a moment.

"He's coming back!" she hissed, then looked around, seeking a weapon she could use to protect herself. Her gaze fell on a battered iron frying pan on the counter. Nancy snatched it up and stationed herself next to the door, well aware that surprise was the only advantage she would have.

A moment later the door crashed open and the guard strode in, his face dark with fury. "What is going on here?" he demanded in Spanish. "Where—"

He got no further, for Nancy brought the frying pan down on the back of his head with all her strength. He dropped heavily to the floor, and Ricardo jumped up, using his ropes to tie the man's wrists and ankles before the burly guard revived.

"Now tell us everything," he said to Nancy. "How did you find us? What is going on at the hacienda?"

Nancy opened her mouth, but no words came out. Suddenly the stress caused by fear, hunger, and lack of sleep swirled around her, and the room began to spin. She was barely conscious of Ricardo's arms, which caught her, or the worried sound of Elena's voice, as she was carried to a blanket in the corner.

"Get her some water," Elena told her fiance.

Nancy tried to sit up.

"Lie still," Elena said. "Are you hurt?"

Nancy took a deep breath, then relaxed for a moment. "I'm okay. Just tired from riding all night and not having anything to eat yesterday," she explained.

"How about some cold tortillas and beans?" Ricardo asked. "It is not the greatest, but if you are really hungry, it helps."

"It sounds heavenly," Nancy admitted, sipping the water, then allowing herself to be helped into a sitting position. "Now tell me how you got here."

"Cordova caught us going into Aunt Rosalinda's room," Elena answered. "He was furious at me for coming back to Colombia, and when I accused him of turning my aunt against me, he called in the guards and they brought us here." Her eyes filled with tears. "They wouldn't listen to me, Nancy. They take orders from him now. They don't even care about Aunt Rosalinda."

"He has been rotating the guards," Ricardo added. "He told me that he wanted the men to be familiar with all parts of the estate, but now I see that he was getting rid of everyone who was loyal to Señora del Luz or to Elena."

Nancy nodded, accepting a plate of beans from the handsome young man. "Cordova seems to be completely in charge, and that Isabella woman is helping him."

Between bites, she told her friends everything she had learned while she'd roamed about the mansion, and about her narrow escape the night before.

Elena gasped. "Rosa Blanca brought you here! She's mine, Nancy. I raised her. Thank goodness you found her to ride. The rest of the burros are half-wild these days. Cordova hates them."

"She found *me*," Nancy corrected. "I knew she had to be a pet when I first saw her at the burro compound. She acted much friendlier than the others. It's a good thing she knew the way to Mesa del Oro."

"I used to come here often as a child," Elena explained. "I liked the place, and sometimes Uncle Jose would let me ride the burro while he followed me in a car."

Nancy smiled, then her expression turned serious again. "We'd better start making plans to—" She stopped as she caught a sound from outside, the whine of a motor laboring up the steep road. "Who's that?" she gasped.

"It must be the other guard," Ricardo replied. "He might have seen the smoke, too."

"What will we do?" Elena asked helplessly.

Nancy looked around the room, aware that they had no time for an elaborate plan. "Could you do what I did, Ricardo?" she asked. "With the frying pan?"

"Of course."

"Then let's get in the chairs, Elena," Nancy said. "Pretend to be tied, and as soon as he stops out in front, start screaming for help as loudly as you can."

Nancy was aware that her friends were looking at her as though she'd lost her senses, but she moved quickly to settle herself in Ricardo's chair. If it was just a single guard coming to take over, she was sure they could handle him as they had the first guard, but if it should be Cordova and his driver . . .

The motor sounds grumbled to a stop, and Nancy looked at Elena. "Now," she hissed.

13

Outwitting the Guard

Elena's screams sent chills along Nancy's spine. They sounded truly terrified. The door burst open and a burly man appeared, his stance ready for attack. His eyes went to Elena, then to Nancy, and Nancy saw the shock in his face. Fearing he'd notice Ricardo if she didn't draw him inside, Nancy yelled and dived sideways off the chair, bumping painfully on the hard-packed earth floor.

"What are you doing here?" the man demanded, stepping inside. "Where is Ricardo?"

"Right here," Ricardo muttered as he swung the frying pan. The man went down as easily as the first guard, and the three young people tied him up beside his colleague.

"Now what?" Ricardo asked, when they were finished.

"We need help," Nancy said.

"What about Aunt Rosalinda?" Elena asked.

"There's no way we can get her out by ourselves," Nancy replied quietly. "Cordova might harm her if we tried."

"But where can we get help?" Ricardo frowned.

"What's the nearest city?" Nancy inquired.

"Cartagena," Ricardo answered.

"Could we get there in the jeep?"

He nodded, then looked at Elena. "Is that what you want to do?"

Elena appeared troubled, but agreed. "It seems our only choice."

"What about them?" Ricardo pointed to the guards.

Nancy shrugged. "Someone will come for them eventually."

The jeep was battered and old, but the gas tank was full, and Ricardo had no trouble starting the engine. As they drove away from Mesa del Oro, he glanced at Nancy. "What do we do in Cartagena?" he asked.

"Go to the police," Nancy suggested.

"No," Ricardo said flatly.

"What do you mean?" The young detective was surprised by his reaction.

"You are in the country illegally," he reminded her.

"I was kidnapped and brought here against my will," she protested.

"So you would tell them," Ricardo said.

"Don't you believe me?" Nancy gasped.

"Of course *I* do," he answered quickly, "but I *know* you, and I was there when you jumped off the plane. That makes a difference."

"Elena was there," Nancy said. "She could vouch for me."

"But you have no proof," Ricardo warned.

"If we all told them . . . " Nancy began, but she had an icy feeling that he was right.

"And what if Señor Cordova were called in?" Elena added. "He would deny everything and accuse us of making trouble. Whom do you think the authorities would believe?"

"But he's done terrible things," Nancy protested.

"He is also a wealthy, respected man, with friends in high places. He came to the hacienda as a highly-esteemed lawyer, not the sort of man that could be suspected of—of whatever it is he's done."

"He's tried to force your aunt to sing a Power

of Attorney that would give him complete control over the del Luz holdings," Nancy exclaimed. "I've seen the paper and heard him talking to Isabella about it. He's in a desperate hurry to take over before you come of age and can challenge him."

"You have no proof of that either," Ricardo pointed out. "And Señora de Luz is certainly in no condition to support your story, is she?"

Nancy had to admit that he was right. "What about the American Consulate?" she suggested. "I'll talk to the officials there and they'll help me reach my father. I'm sure he could convince them to believe me."

Elena shook her head. "You'd never have a chance," she warned.

"What do you mean?" Nancy asked.

"Mr. Dodsworth, the Consul General, is a very good friend of Señor Cordova's. He has even been to the hacienda for visits. He'd never believe you, and he could make it very difficult for you to reach your father."

"But we have to do something," Nancy stated. "We need proof that can make people believe us."

She leaned back and closed her eyes, trying to think. There seemed little hope that she'd find anything in Cartagena that would support her charges against Cordova. Yet, there was the mystery of the ships that had gone down, and she knew that there had to be a connection between them and the hacienda.

"What do you know about the *Rayo del Sol* and the MIC Transport Company?" Nancy asked, then added the names of the other two ships and the companies that owned them.

Ricardo frowned. "I know them. We have used all three firms in the past. I have had little to do with the shipping since my father died about a year ago, but prior to that, I am sure we worked with them. Why?"

Nancy explained about the case she'd been on before her kidnapping. "I don't know what it means or what the connection is, but I do know there must be one. It can't be a coincidence that I was brought to the del Luz hacienda. Cordova knew who I was and he sure was determined to keep me from leaving."

"And you think that the ships weren't carrying the cargo they were supposed to have?" Ricardo asked.

Nancy nodded. "That's the only thing that makes sense. But I don't know how we can tie it all to Cordova."

"Well, he did make his money in shipping," Ricardo said, "but not with any of the companies you named. He had two or three freighters of his own, but he sold them several years ago. However, I am pretty sure of one thing."

"What's that?" Nancy asked.

"Some of the cargo that supposedly went down on those freighters came from the del Luz holdings. I remember hearing the Señora talking about the fact that it had been terribly under-insured and the losses were high."

"So, if Cordova is behind all this, he's been stealing from the estate for some time," Nancy mused.

"He has been running everything since my father's death," Ricardo stated grimly. "And lately the Señora has been in no condition to question his decisions."

"And I was kidnapped because I was poking my nose into the business with the ships," Nancy added.

They drove in silence for a while, then Ricardo slowed down. "We will be in Cartagena soon," he said. "Where do you want to go?"

"Does Cordova have an office in the city?"

"He does," Elena replied. "I went there once with Aunt Rosalinda, before he came to live at the hacienda. I'm sure it's still there. He goes into the city once a week—to take care of his other clients, he says."

"We need to do two things," Nancy decided. "We must investigate the waterfront area and the shipping companies, and we have to get into Cordova's office to examine his files."

"What do you expect to find there?" Ricardo inquired.

"Perhaps a clue that will connect all the loose ends," Nancy replied.

"I think I can get us in," Elena spoke up, her voice becoming excited. "I've been there before, and his assistants should remember me."

"Perhaps I could check out the shipping companies meanwhile," Ricardo volunteered. "Just tell me what you want me to look for. I know some of the employees there. They may be able to help."

"Great," Nancy said. "If we split up, we'll be finished faster."

After discussing Ricardo's approach, Nancy and Elena left him with the jeep near the harbor, planning to take a taxi to the downtown area. While they waited, Nancy looked curiously around. Even her anxiety couldn't keep her from being fascinated by the teeming city they'd entered.

"Beautiful, isn't it," Elena said. "I love to come here and just walk around the old town, visit the churches the Spanish built, look at the ancient buildings and tour the old fortifications in the walls."

She shook her head, her eyes suddenly filled with tears. "Aunt Rosalinda loves it, too. She's the one who told me its colorful history and made me understand what it must have been like when the Spanish built the city and the English and other greedy people attacked it."

"We're doing this to help her," Nancy reminded the girl gently. "If we can find something in Cordova's office that links him to an insurance fraud, we can expose him."

"Right!" Elena said, straightening her shoulders and tossing back her black hair. "What do we do?"

"First tell me everything you remember about his office. What can we expect to find there?"

Elena frowned in concentration. "It's in one of the original houses, a grand place really, which he owns. I only saw the first floor. There's a large reception area with a secretary, then beyond that the library and his private office."

"How many entrances are there to his private office?"

"Well, I went in through the library," Elena mused. "It's behind the receptionist's desk, and she guards it like a tiger. Several legal aides or law students were working in the library at the time, and there were small offices across the hall. My impression was that he has quite a few employees, but I don't really know about the entrances."

"Did you see any files in Cordova's office?"

"Yes, a couple of them between the doors."

"Doors?"

Elena smiled eagerly. "I forgot all about them. There are two. One of them must lead to the side hall."

"A private entrance," Nancy said. "That would be perfect."

"So what do you want me to do?" Elena asked.

"Distract the people who will be in the outer office and library," Nancy answered.

"How?"

"Maybe by doing what would be natural," Nancy said.

"I don't understand," Elena said.

"Suppose you had come from the hacienda and were on your way back to school. You didn't know that Cordova is causing your aunt's strange behavior. Who would you turn to for help?"

Elena's look of disbelief turned to nervous laughter. "You want me to go into his office and ask whoever is there what happened to Aunt Rosalinda?"

"Right. Cry and demand that they do something."

"What if he's there?"

Nancy bit her lip. "Then we're in trouble. But I believe we can assume he won't be. He's tied up at the hacienda looking for me. So get hysterical and keep everybody so busy fussing over you that they won't notice what's going on in his office. Can you do that?"

Elena took a deep breath and nodded. "I'll try my best!" she promised.

14

A Clever Plan

Once they were in a taxi on their way downtown, Nancy pulled a notebook and a pencil out of her purse.

"Can you draw a diagram of Cordova's offices and the rest of the building?" she asked Elena.

The girl nodded and worked on her task while Nancy looked at the city through the window. The old section with its narrow streets was dominated by elegant, two-story townhouses. There were tree-shaded squares cooled by fountains, and the high, white-painted grandeur of the churches built by the Spaniards years ago.

Finally, the taxi drew up in front of an imposing old mansion. "This is it?" Nancy asked Elena.

Her friend nodded and paid the driver.

"It doesn't seem possible that Cordova would be involved in something like insurance fraud if he owns such a splendid estate," Nancy murmured when they got out of the taxi.

"He must be very greedy," Elena agreed. "Now, where do we begin?"

"You go through the front door and start your act," Nancy said.

"What about you?"

"I'll slip around to the back of the house and see if there's a rear entrance. If not, I'll have to get in the front while everyone is busy taking care of you."

Nancy took a couple of steps, then turned back. "Give me a few minutes before you go in," she said.

Elena nodded. Her heart was beating wildly. "How long do you need me to cry and carry on? How will I know when to stop?"

"I'll try to signal you from the hall," Nancy told her. "If you don't see me and you can't continue, just leave and wait for me down the street. I should be able to hear you from the inner office, shouldn't I?"

"Yes," Elena whispered. "Good luck!"

The girls separated in front of the handsome mansion. Nancy moved along the side, using the well-kept shrubs and bushes to hide her. When she got to the back, she smiled in relief. Large French doors gave way to a modern pool area.

The doors stood open and the girl approached them cautiously, tiptoeing across the flagstone patio. Then she peered into the shadowy interior. A gray-haired man stood across the room from her, his attention focused on several papers that were spread out on an old desk.

Nancy watched him bend over the documents, making changes with a pen. Then she heard Elena's scream. It made her jump, even though she had expected it. The man dropped his pen and rushed out a door on the far side of the room.

Cautiously, Nancy stepped inside. This part of the house had not been included in Elena's diagram, since she had never been here. But Nancy had no trouble finding the hall, and from there she reached the door Elena had drawn to Cordova's office. A moment later, she was in the wood-paneled room.

Quickly she opened the first file drawer, her ears ringing with Elena's sobs. Everything was in Spanish, which made her search difficult, but she finally found the folder with the financial statements. Her heart beat with excitement. Here, in front of her, were the names of the shipping lines she had suspected of committing fraud, and documents relating to the insurance payoffs for the three sunken freighters.

Nancy slipped the relevant pages into her purse. Now, if she could only signal Elena that it was time to leave!

Suddenly she stiffened. She no longer heard crying! Quickly Nancy moved to leave the office. But before she could slip out, footsteps approached the library door. "What do you mean, she just left here?" Señor Cordova demanded. "Where did she go?"

In panic, Nancy opened a narrow door closest to her and quickly pulled it shut behind her. For a moment, it was too dark for her to know where she was. Then she felt clothing brush her arm and realized she had taken refuge in a closet.

"Why didn't you keep her here?" she heard Cordova say as he strode into the office, his tone furious.

A woman answered him, explaining that Elena had been very upset about her aunt and finally ran out of the office in despair. The lawyer slammed the door angrily.

Nancy cowered behind two coats, hoping that the man had left the room, but footsteps told her that he was still there. A moment later she heard his voice. "Isabella? Call off the search for the girl and send someone to Mesa del Oro!"

He's on the phone! Nancy thought.

Cordova continued. "Elena was in my office just a few minutes ago. The Drew girl must have escaped and freed her and Ricardo. I believe all three of them are in Cartagena."

There was a short pause, then he went on, "Do not panic, Isabella! Do nothing until I get back. I still have friends who can help. I will make a phone call and then return to the hacienda."

Cordova hung up. After a few moments, Nancy could hear his voice again. "Dodsworth? Cordova here. I have a problem I would like you to help me with." He sounded smooth and oily. "Have you seen anyone wandering into your office today? A young girl, American, with reddish-blond hair and blue eyes?"

Nancy thought grimly that Elena had been right about the American Consul General.

Cordova continued, "She will probably be along before nightfall . . . oh, no, nothing that drastic. I just need twenty-four hours, Jack. If you can keep her from talking to anyone that long, I can get things wrapped up."

Twenty-four hours to do what? Nancy thought. To force Rosalinda del Luz to sign the

Power of Attorney and remove her from the hacienda?

"Well, if I have my way," Cordova spoke again, "you will not see her. I will do my best to take care of everything from this end. But I wanted to cover all my bases. By the way, she is in the country illegally, so you might put the word out that she should be investigated."

There was silence for several moments, then Cordova said good-bye. Shortly after he hung up, Nancy heard the door open and close.

She forced herself to wait five minutes to make sure he had really left, then cautiously peeked out of her closet. The office was empty. Nancy took a deep breath, straightened her shoulders, and walked out.

The hall seemed a mile long, and she felt a nervous twitch between her shoulder blades as she approached the front door, but no one noticed her. The next instant, she stepped out into the bright afternoon sunlight. She'd made it!

The young detective hurried down the street looking for Elena. She had gone nearly two blocks when a soft voice called her name and saw Elena sitting at a small umbrella table in an outdoor cafe.

"What happened?" the dark-haired girl asked as Nancy sank into the chair next to her. "Did he see you?"

Nancy shook her head. "No, but I had to hide in the closet. What about you?"

"When I went into my act, Cordova's secretary called the hacienda. She was informed that he had left and was on his way to town. Isabella thought he'd arrive any minute. I was worried, but carried on some more. Finally I couldn't stand it any longer and left, hoping you would do the same before he got in and caught us."

"I'm glad you did," Nancy said, then told Elena what she had overheard.

"We must warn Ricardo!" Elena said. "Cordova will have a search party out for us now that he knows we're here."

Nancy nodded, well aware of the danger. She had not mentioned the twenty-four hour limit Cordova had given Dodsworth, since she knew Elena was already frightened enough about her aunt.

"Let's get down to the harbor," she said.

Twenty minutes later the girls arrived at the Cartagena office of the MIC Transport Company, where they had agreed to meet Ricardo.

"I'm glad this branch isn't closed," Nancy

said, remembering the shabby, boarded-up office she had tried to visit in San Pedro.

"What will we do?" Elena asked, noticing curious glances from several dockworkers passing by.

Nancy pulled her into the shadows of an alley across from MIC.

"Wait for Ricardo," she answered.

"Why don't I go inside to see if he has arrived yet?" Elena suggested. "If you go, they might become suspicious, but I think I can do it."

Nancy nodded and settled down to wait. After a few moments, a sudden movement far to her right caught her eye. She turned and saw a man coming her way. Her blood chilled as she recognized him as the tall, dark man who had followed her from Phoenix to California.

Just then, Elena came back. "Nancy, Ricardo hasn't been here yet," she reported. "Do you think we should try—"

The girl stopped short when she realized that Nancy was not paying attention to her. Instead, her friend was staring at the man, who by now had almost reached the mouth of the alley. Elena recognized him instantly. She had seen him at the hacienda many times; he worked there.

The man knew her, as well. "Señorita Elena!" he called out, a crooked smile appearing on his tanned face. "How nice to see you here. I have a message for you from Señora del Luz."

"You saw Aunt Rosalinda?" Elena asked.

Nancy heard the hope in the Spanish girl's voice. "It's a trick!" she hissed in her friend's ear. "He's working for Cordova!"

The man quickly came closer. "I really must talk to you, Señoritas!" he said.

"Run!" Nancy shouted.

Elena nodded and plunged through the alley. Nancy was right behind her. "This should take us back to the main street," the Spanish girl panted. "Perhaps we'll find Ricardo there."

Her words ended in a squeal of fear when she realized that two more men were blocking the end of the alley!

15

Trapped

Nancy and Elena stopped running as the three men moved in on them.

"Now we will talk!" the stranger from Phoenix said.

Nancy forced herself to be calm. "What do you want to talk about?" she asked. "Who are you?"

"His name is Juan," Elena said.

"He's the one who kidnapped me and brought me here from Phoenix!" Nancy declared.

"How could you do this?" Elena demanded angrily. "My aunt will fire you for this, Juan!"

The man snorted. "Your aunt is a sick old woman who fires no one!" He gestured to the girls. "You will come with me."

Nancy looked around for help, but the alley

113

was deserted. Juan grabbed her arm in a bruising grip. "Now!" he snarled.

Elena cried out as the other men took her roughly by the hands. They pulled the girls back through the alley and past the MIC office. Suddenly a door in one of the buildings behind it was thrown open, and Nancy and Elena were thrust through it into darkness.

Nancy stumbled and fell when the door crashed closed behind them.

"Elena?" she cried out. "Elena, are you all right?"

There was a scrambling movement and a hand caught at her arm. "Yes, Nancy," her friend whispered.

"Do you have any idea where we are?"

"We're probably in the MIC warehouse," the Spanish girl replied. "When I was in the office, I noticed a door opening into the warehouse behind it."

"That figures," Nancy murmured.

"What are we going to do?" Elena asked.

Nancy pulled the matches out of her pocket and lit one. Its brief flare showed a small, cluttered area with no windows. Then she remembered she still had the candle in her purse. A moment later, a more steady light illuminated their surroundings.

Elena giggled nervously. "It doesn't really improve the scenery," she said.

"No," Nancy agreed. "This place is a mess. I hope Ricardo manages to avoid being caught. But even if he does, he has no idea where we are." She went to the door and tried to open it. As she had expected, it did not budge.

"No doubt Cordova sent out Juan and the other men when he realized we'd be snooping around the harbor," she said gloomily. "Now that he's got us, he can go ahead with his plan."

"Which is?"

"To force your aunt to sign the Power of Attorney, then take over your estate."

"But that can be changed as soon as I'm twenty-one, can't it?" Elena asked. "In a few months I can discontinue his services. He must know that."

"That's right," Nancy said thoughtfully. "Apparently he's not concerned about it. He must be planning something important in the interim."

She sighed. "Let's check out this place. Perhaps we'll find something we can use as a weapon if someone comes for us."

"Like a frying pan," Elena said wryly.

"Don't say that, it reminds me of food!" Nancy was suddenly aware of how hungry she was.

"I know," Elena chuckled. "Even cold beans and tortillas would taste good now."

"Come on, searching will take our minds off our stomachs," Nancy said resolutely as she moved toward the piles of debris that were stacked on all sides. "We might even find another door behind all this junk."

Elena nodded. "It does seem strange that the place would only be accessible from the street, doesn't it?" She headed for a stack of large bales, while Nancy attacked a tarp-covered pile in a far corner. The light was dim, but when she dragged the dirty tarp away she could see that it had covered several small boxes. She bent close to read the words stenciled on the sides.

"Elena!" she called out suddenly. "Come here!"

The girl hurried over and stared at the spot Nancy was pointing to. In the light of the flickering candle, she saw two intertwining circles with the words del Luz written across them.

"The del Luz logo!" she cried out. "That means this shipment is ours!"

"Right," Nancy agreed. "Let's see what's inside. She pulled at the top of one of the boxes and finally managed to break open one end. Inside the carton were beautifully embroidered shawls, each sealed in a plastic bag.

"This is not a new shipment!" Elena declared.

"How can you tell?"

"There's a small village up in the hills where the women have a tradition of making these lovely shawls," Elena replied. "As far as I know, they're the only ones in the whole country who do this kind of work."

"So?"

"Their entire output is about three or four of these boxes per year," Elena continued. "We have not received any for several months. The last shipment was lost at sea—Nancy, it must have been on one of the freighters you're investigating!"

"Except the merchandise wasn't lost at sea at all, it was stashed right here in this warehouse!" Nancy added.

Suddenly a sound at the door claimed their attention. The girls instinctively ducked behind the boxes. The next moment the door flew open and someone was hurled into their prison.

"Ricardo!" Elena cried, her voice breaking with despair.

Ricardo groaned as he rolled over, revealing his battered face. Elena sobbed. "What have they done to you? Are you all right?"

Nancy quickly took a handkerchief out of her purse and handed it to Ricardo, then squatted down beside the young man.

"Can you talk to us?" she asked softly.

Ricardo sat up and grinned. "I am all right. I tried to fight, but I should have known Juan and his playmates would not be easy to get away from." He winced as he took the handkerchief and wiped his split lip and bruised cheek.

"They were waiting for me when I arrived at the MIC office," he went on. "Juan called me over and told me they had seen you both in the area. I thought it might be a trick, but I could not be sure. Señora del Luz trusted Juan, I know she did."

"Now he works for Cordova," Elena said. "I wish I hadn't gone into the MIC office looking for you. Someone probably tipped off Juan that you were coming!"

Nancy agreed, then turned to Ricardo. "Juan is the man who followed me in the United States and kidnapped me."

Ricardo groaned. "I wish I had known. Anyway, I went after him around the corner, and the others were waiting there. I tried to get away, but I was outnumbered."

"Did you learn anything?" Nancy asked.

"Cordova is definitely involved with those shipping lines," Ricardo replied. "When I questioned people at the first firm, no one would speak to me. At the second company, one of the employees I knew told me to forget about the whole thing. 'You will get into trouble asking questions like this,' he said. And I sure did," Ricardo finished with a bitter grin, touching his swollen lip. "How about you two?"

"I can prove that Cordova's the man behind the three corporate names," Nancy said. "He owns the shipping lines, but he remains in the background. He collected insurance on plenty of the cargo."

"Only the cargo was never loaded onto the ships!" Elena added. "We found the shawls that Aunt Rosalinda thought were lost at sea right here!"

"What!"

Nancy pointed to the cartons. "Look for yourself."

Ricardo examined the boxes. "They were supposed to go to an exclusive shop in Beverly Hills, California," he said.

"Do you remember the port they were shipped from?" Nancy asked.

Ricardo nodded. "A place down the coast from here. Obviously, the cargo was brought to Cartagena and unloaded before the ships were sunk, just as you suspected!"

16

Concealed Cargo

"Nancy, I believe you solved your mystery!" Elena spoke up after a moment of silence.

"Not quite," the girl detective replied. "We still don't know how Cordova explained to the insurance companies why the freighters made this unscheduled stop."

"That is easy enough," Ricardo said. "In shipping, it happens often that rush orders have to be picked up from places where the ship had not planned to stop. Sometimes the requests come in after the freighter has already departed its original port."

Nancy nodded. "I see. So Cordova diverted his freighters to Cartagena, since his companies were based here. That way he could unload and stash the cargo in his own warehouses. Then he sank the freighters and collected the insurance not only on the cargo, but on the ships themselves. The records I took from his office indicate that those ships were barely making a profit."

"When he found out that you were checking into the sunken ships," Elena went on, "he became nervous. But I don't understand one thing."

"What's that?" Nancy asked.

"*How* did he find out about your investigation?"

Nancy frowned. "When my father contacted the MIC Transport company by telephone, he spoke to a clerk who promised to relate the message to the man in charge, who would return the call. But the man never did, and subsequent calls were not answered. Apparently word got to Cordova, who promptly closed down the San Pedro office of MIC and his other companies involved in the fraud."

"That makes sense," Ricardo agreed.

"Cordova then sent Juan to scare the Johnsons," Nancy went on. "Dad may have told the man at MIC that he was representing them. Juan was ordered to stay in Phoenix for a while to make sure the threat had worked. He tailed the Johnsons, saw them meet me in the cafe, probably overheard our conversation, and knew we were pursuing the matter."

She shook her head with a sigh. "He got to San Pedro ahead of me, saw me snooping around the harbor, and probably figured I would check with the employment office for crew members of the *Rayo del Sol.* He stationed his buddy, Charlie Sim, there, who sent me on a wild goose chase to Mr. Liu in San Francisco."

Elena, who had heard that part of the story from Nancy before, giggled. "Liu probably never set foot on the *Rayo del Sol,* Nancy."

The girl detective nodded. "No. But he was a good hypnotist. They just didn't count on my seeing Juan afterwards, which jarred my memory and ruined their clever plan."

Nancy paused for a moment, then continued. "Obviously, Juan was supposed to make sure I was going home. When he found out I was stopping off at Phoenix, he figured something had gone wrong. So he kidnapped me and put me on the plane to Colombia."

Elena nodded. "They probably felt they could hold you in the hacienda until Cordova carried out his scheme to get the Power of Attorney from my aunt."

"It all fits," Nancy said. "Except I still have a

feeling that Cordova is up to something that we cannot even guess."

"So what do we do now?" Ricardo asked.

"We should search through the rest of this stuff," Nancy declared. "We had just started before you—arrived so unexpectedly."

Ricardo grimaced.

"We were looking for something we could use as a weapon in case they come for us," Elena told him.

"Good idea," he said. "Let's look." He went across the room to shift crates, boxes, and bales, muttering to himself as he recognized the names of other branches of the vast del Luz holdings. Packing lists were pasted on the containers, and he could tell that none of the cargo would yield any usable weapons.

"Mostly cloth," he reported. "Not a single shipment of hammers or knives or anything we could use to get out of here."

Nancy let herself slide down to the floor, leaning her cheek against her propped up hand. She was tired, hungry, and worried and there seemed to be no way out. For once she had no idea of what to do next.

Her fingers probed the wall next to her. It consisted of wooden boards. Suddenly, she found a rotten one that wiggled. Nancy quickly pulled her metal nail file out of her purse and used it to pry the board away from the others. It was not easy. Ricardo dropped to his knees beside her to help, and finally the board separated from the rest of the wall. Ricardo began to work on the next one, which was also rotting, but the sound of male voices stopped him.

One belonged to Juan! "So what did the boss say?" someone asked him.

"The cargo goes tonight on the *Caviota*. We are to load them after dark." Juan's tone was full of malice. "We do not have to worry about Señorita Snooper or the others for a long time."

"The *Caviota* is not to sink, is it?" the first man asked.

"The *Caviota* is too valuable. It will sail for the Far East," Juan replied. "It will visit several out-of-the-way ports."

Nancy looked at Ricardo and Elena. They realized that *they* were the cargo under discussion. Was Cordova planning to abandon them in an isolated port in the Far East?

"Why does he send the *Caviota* so far away?" the first man asked. "He never ships anything far away from the Americas."

"She is going to a new owner," Juan replied.

"Señor Cordova is selling the freighter?"

"He is trading it for an oil tanker for his newest venture," Juan explained.

"An oil tanker?" Obviously the other man doubted the soundness of that decision. "You joke?"

"No. Do not worry about it." Juan's tone was suddenly chilled. "Just mind that the cargo is safe until nightfall. You need not do anything more. Now come, we have things to take care of."

There were sounds of footsteps retreating, then silence on the other side of the wall.

Nancy sat on the floor, puzzled. "An oil tanker?" she asked after a moment. "What would he want an oil tanker for?"

"It reminds me of something," Ricardo began, his forehead creased in deep concentration. "Several years ago, not long after my father became ill, Señora del Luz told him that she had been contacted by a group of men who were convinced that there was a good chance of finding oil in one of the distant holdings of the estate."

"Oil on the del Luz land?" Elena exclaimed.

Ricardo nodded. "They wanted to drill test-wells."

"Why didn't I hear about this?" Elena asked.

Ricardo shrugged. "As I said, my father was already ill. The men spoke of the high cost of the exploratory drilling, and the Señora told them she was not interested in becoming involved in such an expensive enterprise at that point. It was never mentioned again, as far as I know."

Nancy leaned against the wall, her mind spinning. The new information fit into the puzzle only too well.

"I believe this may be the reason for Cordova's scheme," she said. "Suppose those same people approached him again about the possibility of drilling for oil? What would he do?"

"Authorize it," Ricardo answered without hesitation. "But he would need the Señora's permission."

"Or her Power of Attorney," Elena added.

"It may also explain his need for money," Nancy went on. "He probably would have to share in the financing of the venture, or even carry the cost himself. What better way to make a bundle than to get rid of several marginal freight ships that didn't show a profit and collect the insurance premiums?"

Ricardo nodded. "And that is why he was so worried about your investigation, Nancy. It was not only that you might discover the insurance fraud, but the other deal as well!"

Nancy nodded. "He told Dodsworth that he needed twenty-four hours," she said. "After that, he said, he would have everything wrapped up."

"What!" Elena stared at her, horrified.

"I didn't want to tell you before, because I knew you were worried enough about your aunt. But now we need to think about that."

"It must mean that he feels he can get the Power of Attorney within that time period," Ricardo declared.

"And then he'll send Señora del Luz away and put her under special care," Nancy went on. "I heard him say something like that to Isabella."

"Away from the hacienda?" Elena cried. "Nancy, she will die!"

"So we must stop him!" Nancy said firmly.

"But how?" Ricardo asked.

"Let's work on these wooden boards. If we can pull enough of them away, perhaps we can slip into the other part of the warehouse."

Ricardo turned to the wall without a reply. He knew it was the only hope they had.

17

Slim Hope

Although Nancy and her friends had nothing to work with but their hands, the hole grew rapidly. But the rotten part of the wall extended only a short distance, and their efforts were thwarted by stronger, new boards.

Ricardo groaned. "I will never be able to fit through that hole," he said in despair, as the two girls collapsed beside him. "And we cannot break away the rest without an axe."

"I don't think I can make it through, either," Elena said, trying to wiggle past the splintery opening. A moment later, she cried out in pain and dragged herself back into their prison.

"Did you see anything on the other side?" Nancy asked.

Elena shook her head. "There are packing boxes in the way." She looked appraisingly at Nancy. "You're thinner than I am," she stated. "Maybe you can make it through."

Nancy peered dubiously at the small opening. "I'll try," she said, lying down on the floor. Then she worked her way forward. It was a tight squeeze, and she felt the rough edges of the boards digging into her back as she inched ahead, but a few moments later she was on the other side, faced by a stack of boxes.

She stuck her head back through the hole. "I have an idea of how we can all get away!" she declared.

Ricardo looked at her skeptically. "I will never get through that hole!"

"You don't have to." With that, Nancy wiggled her way back into their prison.

"What are you doing?" Elena stared at her, puzzled.

"I'm going to hide you," Nancy said. "If we can make those men believe that we all got away, they may leave the door open for you to escape."

"I don't get it," Elena said.

Nancy looked around the cluttered room and picked a spot she felt was suitable for her plan. "That corner," she decided. "You hide there, and I'll stack up these crates in front of you so it appears that no one could be behind. Then I'll rig up another stack, attach this string to it, and go through the hole. When I'm on the other side, I'll pull the string. The crates will collapse, and attract the men's attention."

Ricardo shrugged. "It sounds crazy, but it may work." He handed Nancy the keys to the jeep and explained where he had parked it. "If you get away and we don't, take the car."

"Okay," Nancy said, "that's what I had in mind. I'll drive to one of the tourist hotels and contact my Dad from there. If you two manage to get out as well, I'll meet you at the jeep, okay?"

"Okay," Elena said, sounding more courageous than she felt.

"Now flatten yourselves against the wall," Nancy went on, "so I can rig up these boxes."

It took a long while before she was satisfied with her work. But when she was finished, she had arranged the boxes so it appeared that they were stacked flush against the wall. No one could slip behind them and hide. Nancy hoped that would fool the men.

She built a pyramid of crates next to the hole and tied the string she had spotted to a crate in the bottom row. Then she took the other end of the long cord and slipped through the hole. She dropped the string when she was through, and moved along the packing crates to the end of the stack and peered out. What she saw made her heart sink.

A half dozen men were busily working in a large room, carrying in boxes, checking markings, and stacking equipment. There was no sign of Juan. A large door stood open at the side of the building, in line with the door to their prison. Another door straight ahead appeared to lead into the office.

Well, I'll have to risk it, Nancy thought, and retreated to the hole. As she did, her foot brushed against a small object. She bent down and saw a screwdriver that someone had evidently dropped. Quickly Nancy picked it up and slipped it into her pocket.

A moment later she pulled on the string, and the relative quiet of the warehouse was broken by crashing crates.

All work stopped immediately as the men froze, then looked around.

"The prisoners!" Juan yelled, appearing from the office part of the warehouse. "Quick, we must stop them before someone outside comes to investigate the noise."

Nancy held her breath as the men dropped what they were doing and pounded after Juan out the side door. The last of them slammed it shut behind them!

In a flash, Nancy ran to the door. It had automatically locked from the outside! Without wasting time, the girl detective ran through the other door to the office. She had taken no more than a dozen steps when a hand closed on her elbow.

"Where are you going?" a deep voice demanded.

Nancy gulped and whirled around to face a gray-haired man in a business suit. He gazed at her curiously, but there was no hostility in his eyes. Apparently he did not know that Juan had been holding her and her friends captive in the back.

"My dog!" Nancy gasped. "It ran over there!" she pointed toward a distant corner.

The man turned to look. Nancy pulled the screwdriver from her pocket and tossed it in the direction of warehouse, where it landed with a clatter.

"Get him!" she pleaded. "Don't let him get in there, or I'll never find him!"

The man hurried toward the warehouse as Nancy dashed out the front door, dodging past several people. Luckily, no one made an attempt to stop her. There were sounds of turmoil behind her, but she did not look back. She ran until she came close to the jeep.

Elena and Ricardo were not there. Had they managed to escape? Nancy saw a man lounging casually against a nearby tree, looking at the jeep. He appeared to be an aimless drifter, but he was watching the getaway car like a hawk.

Nancy dared not go any further. She backed into the shadow of a doorway. As she did, she felt a hand touch her arm. The girl jumped, and strong hands steadied her.

"What are you waiting for?" Ricardo hissed. "Juan will have a search party after us any minute now."

"He left a guard," Nancy panted, her knees weak with relief as she saw that her friends had escaped, too. "The guy leaning on the tree over there."

"I've seen him around the hacienda," Ricardo whispered. "But he cannot keep us here by himself."

"I'll distract him," Elena said. "I'll go down the alley. He knows me and may follow me. You two get in the jeep and pick me up, okay?"

Nancy nodded. There was no time for further discussion. The man had been so intent on the jeep that he appeared not to have noticed the three young people, but she knew he might look in their direction any moment.

Elena hurried out of the doorway and walked toward the man. He glanced at her, and then, as they had hoped, followed her when she had passed him.

Quickly Ricardo and Nancy jumped into the jeep. Nancy handed the young man the keys, and a moment later he started the engine. The sound made the man look back. He seemed confused, not knowing what to do next. Elena broke out in a run, using his hesitation to put some distance between them. Ricardo drove down the street and came to a screeching stop beside her as Nancy pulled her up before the man had a chance to stop them. Then the jeep was gone, leaving nothing but a cloud of dust.

"Where do you want me to go?" Ricardo asked Nancy tensely.

"Back to the downtown area," Nancy said. "Stop at the first respectable-looking restaurant. I want to phone my father."

Ricardo nodded, and half an hour later, the three friends crowded around a public telephone. Elena told the operator she wanted to place a collect call to River Heights, and was told to hang up and wait.

"I hope it doesn't take too long to get through," Nancy said nervously. "We don't have much time to spare!"

18

Foiled

Nearly fifteen minutes passed before the operator called back and Nancy was able to speak to her father. When he heard her voice, he cried out in relief.

"Nancy! Where are you?"

Quickly she filled him in on what had happened.

Mr. Drew was silent for a moment, then said, "I have a contact in Cartagena through Jules Johnson. A classmate of his is now managing the beach hotel *Triton*. His name is George Rinaldo. I'll call him and tell him you need help. Go see him right away. You will have very little chance of rescuing Rosalinda del Luz on your own."

"Yes, Dad," Nancy said, and hung up without wasting any more precious time. She told her friends what Mr. Drew had suggested, and Ricardo smiled. "I know where the *Triton* is. I will drive you there."

The sun was beginning to set when the young people pulled up in front of the elegant hotel. They felt self-conscious about their battered jeep but were in too much of a hurry to find another spot.

"We don't look too great, either," Nancy said, glancing at her dirty jeans and sweater.

Ricardo grinned ruefully. "I will wait in the car," he decided. "When people see me with my battered face, they are liable to call the police!"

"Good idea," Nancy said. "Come on, Elena."

The two girls went through the revolving door and approached the clerk behind the desk. "I would like to speak to Mr. Rinaldo, please," Nancy told him.

The man stared at her for a moment. "Er, Mr. Rinaldo is not here right now," he replied. "If you will take a seat over there," he said, nodding toward several sofas and armchairs in the middle of the lobby, "I will find out when he is expected."

He disappeared through a door leading into

an office right behind him. Nancy and Elena were too anxious to sit down. They waited nervously for him to come back.

A young woman in a blue and white uniform, one of the hotel workers, strode through the lobby, slipped behind the counter, and entered the office. She left the door open while she walked to a file on the far left.

Nancy and Elena could here the clerk talking, although his words were muffled, but did not see him. Suddenly Nancy stiffened. At the same moment, Elena grabbed her hand. Both had overheard the name Dodsworth!

Nancy pulled Elena away from the desk. "Come on!" she hissed, and the girls hurried outside. They jumped into the jeep and Nancy cried, "Let's go, Ricardo! Hurry!"

Ricardo asked no questions until they had put several miles between themselves and the *Triton Hotel*. Then he turned to Nancy. "Now tell me what this was all about?"

"When Cordova checked out Mr. Johnson in Phoenix, he must have done an extremely thorough job," Nancy replied. "Obviously, he learned that Johnson had a friend in Cartagena—Mr. Rinaldo, who may or may not have been at the *Triton* when we arrived. If he was, I'm sure the clerk didn't tell him about us.

Anyway, either Dodsworth, or Cordova pretending to be Dodsworth, called the hotel and alerted the clerk to look out for an American girl who may ask for Mr. Rinaldo."

"We heard the clerk in the office mention the name Dodsworth," Elena took up the story. "He was probably phoning the police, asking them to come arrest us because Nancy is in the country illegally."

Ricardo bit his lip. "I have friends who live about sixty miles away from the city," he said. "Perhaps we could go there."

"Can you call them?" Nancy asked.

Ricardo shook his head. "Their number is unlisted and I do not have it with me."

"Do they live on the way to the hacienda?" the girl detective went on.

"No, their home is in the other direction."

Nancy stared into the falling dusk. "We don't have time," she decided. "We must go back to the hacienda and try to rescue Rosalinda del Luz ourselves. How long will it take us?"

"We know a shortcut," Elena spoke up. "It's a rough road, but it saves about an hour. We should be able to make it in an hour and a half."

"Okay," Nancy said.

Ricardo raced through the heavy traffic to a serenade of blaring horns and screeching tires.

Half an hour later he turned off the main highway.

The ride was worse than Nancy had expected. The road was no more than two ruts in the ground that disappeared on rocky ridges and tormented their weary, aching bodies. They passed through deserted woods and fields, and never spotted a human being during the entire trip.

Darkness had long fallen when Nancy finally asked, "Is it much farther?"

"No," Ricardo replied. "Only a few more minutes."

"Where does this road end?"

"At the gate."

"We can't go in that way!" the young detective objected. "We'll have to enter the way I came out."

"That would take too long," Ricardo said. "We will go through the caves."

"The caves?" Nancy asked.

"There are tunnels and underground vaults inside the cliffs," Elena explained. "When we were children, we used to play there and explore the passages."

"Good!" Nancy was relieved, as Ricardo turned off the rutted road and plunged into the trees. Branches scraped at the sides of the jeep, but he did not dare use the headlights, inching forward by the dim glow of his parking lights.

"Will we be able to see our way in the caves?" Nancy asked.

"We always left candles in there," Elena replied. "I don't suppose anyone has taken them."

"I still have matches," the girl detective declared, putting her hand in her pocket to make sure that they had not fallen out.

"Here they are."

Suddenly a series of sharp reports penetrated the stillness. The jeep quivered, then plunged forward, bounding and twisting, before it came to a stop near a tree.

"What was that?" Elena gasped.

"Somebody heard us and fired shots," Ricardo whispered, pulling the girls down low. "He must have hit a tire."

Several more shots rang out, but found no target.

"We have to get out of here!" Nancy said urgently. "Eventually they'll find the jeep!"

"Yes," Ricardo said. "Just try to stay as close to the ground as you can. The entrance is not far from here."

He took the girls by the hands and led them through the dim forest, toward the deep shadows of the cliffs. Nancy held her breath as they left the shelter of the trees and climbed up the slippery rock to an opening about fifteen feet off the ground. It was camouflaged by low bushes, and she marveled that Ricardo found it without a search. Once inside, they collapsed on the rocky ground.

"We made it!" Elena exclaimed.

"But they know we are here, and will be looking for us," Ricardo warned. "It will not be easy to get into the house." He felt around in a crevice and produced two fat candles. "These have been here for years," he said. "I hope they will still burn."

Nancy pulled out her matches. She had trouble lighting the dusty, damp candles, but succeeded after several attempts. A moment later, the trio moved cautiously into the depths of the cave.

Their climb was a nightmare as they made their way through rough, often sliding, shifting rocks that rattled ominously behind them. Ricardo set a quick pace, but neither Nancy nor Elena tried to slow him. Finally he came to a stop.

"We must blow out the candles now," he declared.

"Where are we?" Nancy whispered.

"Just around the corner from the exit," Elena replied. "We come out in the burro pasture."

A moment later, they found themselves in pitch darkness. Holding on to one another, they pressed forward until Nancy could make out the shape of an opening concealed by heavy brush. The rays of a nearly full moon helped them to see the exit. They emerged into the cool night air with sighs of relief.

"Now comes the hard part," Ricardo warned, as he surveyed the hacienda in the distance. Searchlights were sweeping the grounds from the walls, and Cordova's men could be seen as they patrolled the estate.

The young people crept cautiously toward the house. Twice the light almost caught them, but finally they reached the sanctuary of the heavy vines that covered the hidden door. Once inside the tunnel, Nancy lit the two candles again. "I'll be out of matches soon," she said worriedly.

"Perhaps we will find some in the Señora's room," Ricardo said.

"If we ever get there," Elena added, her voice not too steady.

Nancy pressed her friend's hand. "We will!" she said firmly. "We have to!"

Ricardo led the way to the foyer closet. "I would feel better if I knew Cordova was in his office before we go upstairs," he said.

When they came to the closet door, he cracked it open cautiously and looked out. "The light is on in the office," he whispered. "Come on!"

Silently the young people slipped out of the closet and tiptoed up the stairs. No one was in the second floor hallway, and they hurried to Elena's aunt's room. It appeared to be quiet, so they went in.

But when they stepped up to the bed, they gasped. *Rosalinda del Luz was gone!*

19

Where is the Señora?

"We're too late!" Elena cried.

"Where could they have taken her?" Ricardo asked.

"I don't know—" Nancy stopped short when they heard footsteps outside. "Someone's coming!" she hissed. "Quick, under the bed!"

All three instantly dived under the large, canopied bed. A moment later, the door opened.

"She's sleeping," Isabella said. "You must not wake her, Señor Cordova. She was very upset about signing the paper. She did not want to take her pills."

"We must get her away from here," Cordova muttered. "Those snoopers are somewhere in the area, and I do not trust them. The plane is ready. You will take her to the sanitarium. Tell them she is deranged, and make sure they do not believe any of her wild tales."

"But, Señor . . . " Isabella's voice trailed off.

"Where is she?" Cordova demanded a second later.

"She was here less than an hour ago," Isabella replied. "I went to make the sandwiches for the guards and—"

"You idiot!" the man screamed. "Where is she?"

"You told the servants to go," Isabella wailed. "You ordered me to make the food. I had to leave her!"

There were sounds of something breaking, then Cordova's bellowed accusations. Isabella's replies were just as loud and furious.

"We must find her," the man finally declared. "Do you have any idea where she could have gone?"

"She asked for Ciomara several times during the last few days," Isabella said after a moment's hesitation.

"What did she want from the old woman?" Cordova demanded.

"Ciomara was her personal servant for many years," Isabella replied. "Perhaps she felt that Cio was the only person she could trust."

"Cio lives at the end of the east wing," Cordova said. "How could the Señora have gone so far?"

"I do not know," Isabella replied. "But she refused to take her sedative tonight. Perhaps she had more strength than we thought."

"All right!" the man stormed. "We will look!" A moment later, the door slammed.

Nancy and her friends emerged from their hiding place. "Do you think that's where your aunt has gone?" Nancy asked Elena.

"It's possible," the girl declared. "I know a quick way to get there—through the secret panel in the alcove."

"But that just leads to a room!" Nancy objected.

"There's another exit from the room that connects to the underground passages," Elena said. "Come on!"

The trio rushed out and flew down the hall. Elena pressed the button on the panel behind the tapestry, and a moment later they stepped into the small, cluttered room where Nancy had found the emerald-eyed cat.

Quickly Nancy lit one of her candles. Then Elena let out a muffled cry. On the floor lay Rosalinda del Luz, her fragile body curled up like a sleeping child's. The golden cat was cradled in her arms!

Nancy dropped to her knees and reached out

to touch the woman's pale cheek.

"Is she . . . ?" Elena asked, her face drawn with fear.

Nancy felt for Rosalinda's pulse and found it steady and slow. "She's all right," the girl said. "Don't worry, she's just exhausted."

"We have to get her away from here!" Elena urged. "She needs medical care. Nancy, what are we going to do?"

"The jeep is not running," Ricardo pointed out. "And we cannot *carry* her to the next hospital."

"Cordova mentioned that the plane was ready," the young detective said. "I have a pilot's license."

"So do I," Ricardo said. "I also know the plane. But how will we get there? It is beyond the gate, and we will never escape past the guards."

"How did you bring me here after I was kidnapped?" Nancy inquired.

"Through the orchard gate," Elena replied. "But that will be patrolled, as well."

"Then we have to get rid of the guards," Nancy declared. "How about the landing strip? Who will be there?"

"I believe only the pilot and the copilot," Ricardo answered. "They usually wait in the hangar office until they are needed to take off."

"If we can think of a way to get the guard away from the orchard gate, can you carry the Señora to the plane?" Nancy asked the young man.

"Yes," he replied.

"I have an idea!" Elena exclaimed suddenly, her dark eyes sparkling.

"What?" Nancy stared at her friend.

"If we could set off the alarm somehow, it would bring the guards running into the house, wouldn't it?"

"Alarm?" Nancy asked.

Elena nodded. "Several years ago, there was a fire in the kitchen. It wasn't much, but Aunt Rosalinda was terribly upset and had smoke alarms installed in the kitchen, the office, and several other places in the main living area."

"That's right!" Ricardo exclaimed. "I remember she rigged them to a siren on the roof in case no one was in the house when there was an emergency. I don't know whether all the guards would respond, but I suspect most of them would."

Nancy smiled. "Then we'll use it!" she said confidently.

"But how?" Elena's face suddenly fell. "I don't want to burn down the hacienda just so the alarms will go off."

"That's no problem," Nancy said. "You don't need a big fire to set off a smoke alarm. I'll take care of it."

"What are you going to do?" Ricardo wanted to know.

"Trust me," Nancy said. "We have no time to waste. I'd like you and Elena to take the Señora and get as close as you can to the orchard gate. How long will that take you?"

"Ten to fifteen minutes," Ricardo replied.

"Good. I'll wait that long before triggering the alarm."

"What if Cordova and Isabella are back by then?" Elena asked worriedly. "It's not that far to Ciomara's room in the east wing."

Nancy frowned. "I know that's a strong possibility. But there are only two of them, and I hope I can avoid them. Where are the other smoke alarms located?"

"One is in the first floor storage room, but that's kept locked most of the time," Elena said. "There's another one at the far end of the house, but you'll never make it all the way there without being seen."

Nancy nodded. "Okay. You two leave now?"

"What about you?" Elena's voice was shaky again.

"I'll try to make it. If I can't, don't let them

catch you." She rummaged in her purse and pulled out a business card. "Here's my father's address and phone number. The minute you land, call him and tell him what happened. I can dodge Cordova and Isabella for a few days by using the secret passage."

"I'll stay and help you!" Elena offered.

"No. You take care of your aunt and help Ricardo get her on the plane. Hurry!"

Ricardo lifted the sleeping woman into his arms, and Elena took the emerald-eyed cat. She walked to the far end of the room and pushed a hidden button. Part of the wall opened into another passageway.

"Nancy," Ricardo said before he went through it, "the orchard gate is to the right of the burro pasture. Go past the stables and you'll find the path that leads there. From the gate, it continues straight to the landing strip."

The girl nodded. "I'll wait ten minutes, then I'll try the alarm in the kitchen."

"Good luck!" Elena said. A moment later, the two had disappeared.

20

Flight to Freedom

Nancy looked at her watch, counting the minutes as they ticked by. No sounds penetrated into her hiding place, and she had no idea where her enemies were at that moment.

Finally, it was time for her to leave. Cautiously she opened the panel behind the tapestry and stepped out. The hallway was empty. Nancy tiptoed to the stairs and stopped to listen. Then she descended silently, slipping into the closet at the bottom of the staircase for temporary shelter. Again she listened carefully. The house appeared to be deserted.

Courage, Nancy told herself. This simply has to work, or we are all lost! She crept out of the closet and made her way to the kitchen. The door stood open, and there was no one inside. Nancy spotted the smoke alarm on the ceiling. But then her heart fell. The device was disconnected!

Of course, the girl thought. It probably went off so many times in this room that someone just pulled out the wire. Now what'll I do?

She stepped behind the doorway and peered out. There was still no sign of Cordova or Isabella. "I'll have to try the office," Nancy said to herself, and resolutely walked to the now familiar door.

She listened for any telltale noise, then slowly turned the doorknob. Cordova was not there! With a sigh of relief, the girl detective slipped inside and closed the door behind her. The light was on and she saw the smoke alarm was right over the desk. Nancy took some paper from a drawer and looked for matches. Luckily, she found two packets on top of a folder. She took them and opened the folder.

"Oh!" A small cry escaped from her lips as she stared at the signed Power of Attorney inside the folder. "Just what I wanted!" Quickly she put the document into her purse, then rolled the blank paper into a tight cylinder and set one end of it on fire. She climbed on top of the desk and held her torch under the alarm. Smoke curled up from the burning paper and drifted into the device. But nothing happened!

Oh, no! Nancy thought. Maybe this one doesn't work, either. She stood with bated breath, terrified that the door might open and Cordova would walk in.

Suddenly, a shrill noise pierced the still air. Nancy almost stumbled off the desk, then she quickly climbed down, extinguished her torch in the metal wastepaper basket, and ran out of the room. A moment later, she was back in the closet.

By now the siren on the roof had begun to wail loudly. I'd better get out of here, Nancy thought, and she hurried through the secret tunnel to the outside door. She opened it a crack and listened. She could hear men running toward the house, shouting in confusion. After a few moments, they had all disappeared, and Nancy slipped outside.

She waited a few seconds, then ran toward the stables as fast as she could. Several times she was caught in the beam of the moving searchlights, but no one noticed her. She found the path to the orchard gate and ran along it, when suddenly she heard a shout in front of her. She dived into a thicket of shrubs, hoping she had not been seen.

There was another shout, and then approaching footsteps. Two men raced past her, talking to each other as they went, wondering what had happened. A moment later, they were gone.

It's a good thing I didn't get to the gate any sooner, Nancy thought, or I would have run straight into their arms!

She stood up and continued along the path, this time more slowly and cautiously, just in case another guard was still there. Soon she saw the gate looming in front of her, with no sign of anyone near it.

She paused a moment and listened, but all was quite. Then Nancy shot through the gate. Her breath was coming in gasps and her right side throbbed with a sharp pain as she ran toward the landing strip.

She paused a moment and listened, but all was quiet. Then Nancy shot through the gate. Her breath was coming in gasps and her right side throbbed with a sharp pain as she ran toward the landing strip.

Suddenly someone yelled, "You there, girl. Stop!"

Nancy looked over her shoulder and saw a man chasing after her. He did not appear to be armed. All at once something shot out of the brush in front of him.

The man tripped and fell, hitting his head and yelling out in pain.

Nancy stared at the scene, frozen to the spot. Then she saw Maro running away from the man toward her, limping slightly.

Instantly Nancy scooped up the black cat and hurried on. She could hear the airplane engines before she saw the craft outlined in the moonlight. With a last spurt of energy, she raced toward it.

"Nancy!" Elena cried, waving from the cabin. The girl detective pushed the cat inside, then held out her hand for Elena to pull her in. A moment later the door slammed shut and the plane quivered before roaring forward. It bounced on the rough turf, gathered speed, and finally lifted off the ground.

Nancy lay on the cabin floor, panting. When she had finally recovered enough to speak, she told Elena how she had managed to escape.

"I'm so glad you made it," the Spanish girl whispered. "We were worried about you." She pointed to a row of seats. "Aunt Rosalinda never woke up. She must have been drugged so heavily that even though she didn't take her sedative tonight, she's sleeping like a baby."

Nancy nodded. "What happened to the pilot and copilot?" she asked.

Ricardo, who heard her question over the din of the engines, chuckled. "I locked them in the office!" he called out. "They will have quite a bit of explaining to do when Cordova finds them."

"Where do we go now?" Elena asked. Ricardo just headed northeast, waiting for further instructions.

"Will you get into trouble if you fly across the Caribbean Sea to the United States without a flight plan?" Nancy inquired.

"It is not allowed, and it's very dangerous," Ricardo replied. "But we have no choice. I did not want to contact any of the Colombian airports because Cordova will undoubtedly report the plane stolen. As soon as I get near one of the Caribbean islands, I will check in and explain what happened. If we are lucky, we will receive clearance to continue on to the United States. Where would you like us to land?"

"How about Phoenix?" Nancy suggested. "Do you have enough fuel to make it there?"

"I think so."

"When you check in for clearance, just tell the authorities to contact my father. He will be able to arrange for us to land safely in Phoenix."

"Then the nightmare will be over," Elena said quietly.

Getting clearance and contacting Carson Drew was more difficult than they had expected, but finally they succeeded. When they arrived at the Phoenix airport, an ambulance was waiting for Rosalinda del Luz. The authorities had contacted the Colombian government regarding Cordova and his partners in crime.

Jules Johnson and his wife took the young people to their home in the suburbs, and the three slept until noon the following day. Mr. Drew had arrived by then, and at dinner they all discussed the trio's adventure, while Maro, the cat, sat contentedly at Elena's feet.

"A man named Juan contacted you," Nancy said to Mr. Johnson, "and threatened you so you would drop the investigation, didn't he?"

Mr. Johnson looked sad. "Yes," he replied. "I knew I was up against people who would stop at nothing. Juan told me that his group had my friend, George Rinaldo, in Cartagena, under close surveillance. If I didn't drop my snooping, as he called it, harm would come to George and his family. There was nothing I could do about it, and I felt I had to protect George."

"I understand," Nancy said.

"I was really worried when you went to Los Angeles," Mr. Johnson went on. "But Juan said that if I told you and your father about him, my wife would be hurt. I had no idea how he learned that I called Carson, but since he had, I just could not risk any further communication with you. When we met in the restaurant, I knew he would be there, eavesdropping on our conversation."

Mrs. Johnson nodded. "That's why we tried to talk you out of continuing your investigation, Nancy. We were hoping Juan would hear us and leave us alone. We just had to end this nightmare!"

"You did the right thing," Mr. Drew assured his friends. "Unfortunately, Juan followed Nancy and finally kidnapped her. But he was no match for her in the end!" He glanced proudly at his daughter and squeezed her hand.

"Thank goodness he wasn't!" Elena spoke up. "And even though it was horrible for Nancy to be kidnapped, it turned out great for us. She saved not only my aunt, but our property, from that evil Cordova!"

Nancy smiled. "I had some wonderful help from Elena and Ricardo," she said. Then she bent down to pick up the cat. She stroked his sleek fur. "And Maro came to my rescue several times. I wouldn't even have gotten on the plane without him!"

Several days later, Rosalinda del Luz was released from the hospital. Elena and Ricardo went to pick her up, while the others prepared a luncheon celebration for her.

When the guest of honor walked into the room, Nancy stared at her in surprise. The lovely, self-assured woman bore little resemblance to the frail creature they had rescued in Colombia!

"So you are the brave girl Elena has been telling me about," Rosalinda said, and embraced the young detective. "My! You do look like Mariposa, don't you. When I was ill, I had a dream that my sister had come back to me—" Rosalinda stopped and stared at Nancy. "It wasn't a dream, was it. It was you!"

"Yes, it was," Nancy replied. "But at the time, you didn't believe me."

"It was horrible," Rosalinda murmured. "They drugged me, and everything was so confusing. I knew they were up to no good, but there was nothing I could do about it."

Elena hugged her aunt. "It's over now. Try to forget all the terrible things that happened."

"They made me believe that you had turned against me!" Rosalinda went on, tears welling up in her eyes. "And Ricardo, too! And when you did not come to see me, I believed them!"

"You had no choice," Elena said. "We know you didn't."

Just then, Mr. Drew came into the room. After greeting their guest, he said, "I have good news from Cartagena. Cordova has been captured and much of what he took from you has been recovered."

"What about my treasures?" Rosalinda asked. "The ones he stole before I hid the emerald-eyed cat from him?"

"If you mean the unicorn and the parrot, they have been found," Mr. Drew replied. "There were also a number of paintings and several valuable antique clocks that a woman named Ciomara identified as belonging to you."

Rosalinda smiled. "Cio was the only person who remained loyal to me during all this. But she was too old and sick to be of any help."

She paused a moment, then said, "You have done so much for me. How can I ever thank you for it?"

"We could invite everyone to the hacienda for a *real* visit," Elena suggested.

"Perhaps for our wedding," Ricardo added, taking his fiance's hand.

"It would be an honor to have you," Rosalinda said to the Drews. "Will you come?"

"We'd be delighted," Mr. Drew replied, and Nancy agreed enthusiastically. "And now, listen to the last bit of news I have."

All eyes turned to him expectantly.

"Among the papers that were found in Cordova's files, the authorities discovered proof that he had begun to drill on your land, Señora."

Nancy stared at her father and saw the sparkle in his eyes. Before she could ask any questions, Mr. Drew continued, "They struck oil, and several companies are eager to bid for the right to develop the field. Señor Cordova has done you a very large favor in his greed!"

After the cheering had died down, Rosalinda said with an impish smile, "I hope he knows about it. But I don't believe I'll bother to thank him for his efforts!" She turned to Nancy. "You're the one who deserves our gratitude."

The young detective blushed. She was thrilled that her adventure in Colombia had such a happy ending, but suddenly she wondered if there would ever be another case for her to tackle. She did not have to worry, because soon she would discover *The Eskimo's Secret*.

"Oh!" she said suddenly, startled out of her pensive mood. Maro had jumped into her lap and stared at her with his big, green eyes. "Meow!" he said.

Nancy laughed and hugged the beautiful cat. "You've been wonderful," she said to him. "I herewith bestow upon you the title of honorary detective!"

JOIN NANCY DREW
AT THE COUNTRY CLUB!

You can be a charter member of Nancy Drew's River Heights Country Club™— Join today! Be a part of the wonderful, exciting and adventurous world of River Heights, USA™.

You'll get four issues of the Country Club's quarterly newsletter with valuable advice from the nation's top experts on make-up, fashion, dating, romance, and how to take charge and plan your future. Plus, you'll get a complete River Heights, USA, Country Club™ membership kit containing an official ID card for your wallet, an 8-inch full color iron-on transfer, a laminated bookmark, 25 sticker seals, and a beautiful enamel pin of the Country Club logo.

It's a retail value of over $12. But, as a charter member, right now you can get in on the action for only $5.00. So, fill out and mail the coupon and a check or money order now. *Please do not send cash.* Then get ready for the most exciting adventure of your life!

THE HARDY BOYS ᴿ SERIES
By Franklin W. Dixon

	ORDER NO.	PRICE	QUANTITY
NIGHT OF THE WEREWOLF—#59	#62480-6	$3.50	
MYSTERY OF THE SAMURAI SWORD—#60	#95497-0	$3.50	
THE PENTAGON SPY—#61	#95570-5	$2.95	
THE APEMAN'S SECRET—#62	#62479-2	$3.50	
THE MUMMY CASE—#63	#41111-X	$3.50	
MYSTERY OF SMUGGLERS COVE—#64	#41112-8	$3.50	
THE STONE IDOL—#65	#42290-1	$2.50	
THE VANISHING THIEVES—#66	#42292-8	$3.50	
THE OUTLAW'S SILVER—#67	#42337-1	$2.50	
DEADLY CHASE—#68	#62477-6	$3.50	
THE FOUR-HEADED DRAGON—#69	#42341-X	$3.50	
THE INFINITY CLUE—#70	#62475-X	$3.50	
TRACK OF THE ZOMBIE—#71	#42349-5	$3.50	
THE VOODOO PLOT—#72	#42351-7	$3.50	
THE BILLION DOLLAR RANSOM—#73	#42355-X	$3.50	
TIC-TAC-TERROR—#74	#42357-6	$3.50	
TRAPPED AT SEA—#75	#42363-0	$3.50	
GAME PLAN FOR DISASTER—#76	#42365-7	$3.50	
THE CRIMSON FLAME—#77	#42367-3	$3.50	
CAVE-IN—#78	#42369-X	$3.50	
SKY SABOTAGE—#79	#47557-6	$3.50	
THE ROARING RIVER MYSTERY—#80	#49721-9	$3.50	
THE DEMON'S DEN—#81	#49723-5	$3.50	
THE BLACKWING PUZZLE—#82	#49725-1	$3.50	
THE SWAMP MONSTER—#83	#55048-9	$3.50	
REVENGE OF THE DESERT PHANTOM—#84	#49729-4	$3.50	
THE MYSTERY OF THE SPACE SHUTTLE—#85	#49731-6	$3.50	
THE HARDY BOYS ᴿ GHOST STORIES	#50808-3	$3.50	
NANCY DREW ᴿ THE HARDY BOYS ᴿ			
BE A DETECTIVE ™ MYSTERY STORIES:			
THE SECRET OF THE KNIGHT'S SWORD—#1	#49919-X	$3.50	
DANGER ON ICE—#2	#49920-3	$2.95	
THE FEATHERED SERPENT—#3	#49921-1	$3.50	
SECRET CARGO—#4	#49922-X	$3.50	
THE ALASKAN MYSTERY—#5	#54550-7	$2.95	

MEET THE

The exciting new soap-opera series

DREAM GIRLS™ is the enchanting new series that has all the glamour of the Miss America Pageant, the intrigue of Sweet Valley High, and the chance to share the dreams and schemes of girls competing in beauty pageants.

In DREAM GIRLS™ you will meet Linda Ellis, a shy, straightforward beautiful girl entering the fast-paced world of beauty contests. Vying for the limelight with Linda is Arleen McVie who is as aggressive, devious and scheming as she is attractive. Join Linda and Arleen as they compete for the scholarships, the new wardrobes, the prizes, the boyfriends

...rds and the glitz of being number one.

Come share the dream as you join the DREAM GIRLS™
backstage in their quest for fame and glory.

#1 **ANYTHING TO WIN**
#2 **LOVE OR GLORY?**
#3 **TARNISHED VICTORY**
#4 **BOND OF LOVE**
#5 **TOO CLOSE FOR COMFORT**
#6 **UP TO NO GOOD**

Archway Paperbacks
Published by Pocket Books,
A Division of Simon & Schuster, Inc.

414

_____ Jim Razzi 63240/$2.50

_____ **MONSTER OF LOST VALLEY: DOUBLE DINOMITE #1**
    Jim Razzi 62091/$2.50

_____ **ESCAPE FROM SKULL ISLAND: DOUBLE DINOMITE #2**
    Jim Razzi 62092/$2.50

Simon & Schuster Mail Order Department MMM
200 Old Tappan Rd., Old Tappan, N.J. 07675

Please send me the books I have checked above. I am enclosing $_____ (please add 75¢ to cover postage and handling for each order. N.Y.S. and N.Y.C. residents please add appropriate sales tax). Send check or money order--no cash or C.O.D.'s please. Allow up to six weeks for delivery. For purchases over $10.00 you may use VISA: card number, expiration date and customer signature must be included.

Name _____

Address _____

City _____ State/Zip _____

VISA Card No. _____ Exp. Date _____

Signature _____ 501